KUNJIKKALI'S
ECHOES OF LIBERATION

Titles by the Same Author

1. *Kunjikkalikkurava* (Malayalam), 2022
2. *Auld Lang Syne*, 2022

KUNJIKKALI'S ECHOES OF LIBERATION

THE MYSTIC STORY OF A DALIT WOMAN RISING ABOVE DEATH

TRANSLATED FROM THE MALAYALAM   A NOVEL

JAYALEKSHMI

KONARK

Konark Publishers Pvt. Ltd
206, First Floor,
Peacock Lane, Shahpur Jat,
New Delhi - 110 049
+91-11-4105 5065
india@konarkpublishers.com, us@konarkpublishers.com
www.konarkpublishers.com

Copyright © Prof. Jayalekshmi, 2025

Originally published in Malayalam as *Kunjikkalikkurava: Kaalathe Velluvillicha Oru Dalit Streeyude Vimochana Veeragadha - Oru Novel* (കുഞ്ഞിക്കാളിക്കുരവ: കാലത്തെ വെല്ലുവിളിച്ച ഒരു ദളിത് സ്ത്രീയുടെ വിമോചന വീരഗാഥ – ഒരു നോവൽ) by Green Books, Kerala, in 2022.

This work was translated into English by the author.

All rights reserved. No part of this book may be reproduced or utilised in any form or by any means, electronic or mechanical, including photocopying, recording, or by any information storage and retrieval system, without prior written permission from the author or the publisher. The views and opinions expressed in this book are solely those of the author. While the accuracy of the facts, as reported by the author, has been verified to the fullest extent possible, the publisher shall not be held liable in any way for the content.

This is a work of fiction. While references may be made to actual events or existing locations, the names, characters, places and incidents are products of the author's imagination. Any resemblance to actual persons, living or dead, businesses, events, or locales is purely coincidental.

ISBN: 978-81-973432-5-4

Edited by Gia Fernandes
Jacket design by Sourish Mitra
Cover and inside illustrations © Prasannan Anickad
Typeset by Saanvi Graphics, Noida
Printed and bound in India by Thomson Press India Ltd.

Dedicated to
Mother Bhageerathi
Mother Lake Sasthamcotta

Contents

Renowned Authors Respond	ix
Gratitude	xi
Prologue	xiii
One	1
Two	12
Three	17
Four	26
Five	34
Six	43
Seven	48
Eight	54
Nine	58
Ten	64
Eleven	71
Twelve	76
Thirteen	84
Fourteen	89
Fifteen	96
Sixteen	106
Seventeen	111
Eighteen	123
Nineteen	130
Twenty	145
Twenty-one	152
Twenty-two	160
Twenty-three	168
Twenty-four	178
Twenty-five	184
Epilogue	191
About the Author	195

Renowned Authors Respond

A powerful indictment of the social inequities of rural India and a moving story of a Dalit woman's lone fight for empowerment, self-assertion and absolution, *Kunjikkali's Echoes of Liberation* is an affecting work. Prof. Jayalekshmi has written a deeply evocative and searing novel of rural Kerala.

—**Dr SHASHI THAROOR**
Member of Parliament (Lok Sabha) | Author

Here is an enchanting narrative of love and rebellion set in a critical context in Kerala's history, of the Renaissance that liberated the Malayali society from several bonds of oppression based especially on class and caste. Kunjikkali, the female protagonist, while representing the oppressed class is also the symbol of their profound awakening that later led to the end of feudal rule and its inhuman practices in the state. But the work is much more than history; it is a tale that carries a range of emotions, from love to rage, from the pain of bondage to the exhilaration of freedom. Prof. Jayalekshmi has succeeded in capturing the spirit of the original in her lucid translation.

—**K. SATCHIDANANDAN**
Poet | Critic | President, Kerala Sahitya Akademi

This is the story of Kunjikkali—a Dalit woman who lived far ahead of her time. Her life unfolds as an anatomy of love in all its forms—enduring, eternal, and heartbreaking. From loyalty to rebellion, her tale captures the struggles of the humble against the powerful. Kunjikkali's ululation is not just a cry of celebration, but a powerful protest for freedom—a voice that echoes through the rich, turbulent history of Travancore, from the 1940s to the 70s. Love, self-reliance, resistance and spirited fight for survival entwine in this gripping story.

—**TUHIN A. SINHA**
Author | Politician | Content Strategist

An enthralling story of a defiant Dalit woman. Kunjikkali's life is a powerful blend of love, rebellion, and the quest for freedom, echoing through her heart-wrenching ululation haunting the readers till the very end, and thereafter. Prof. Jayalekshmi's visually rich narrative takes the reader on a profound and evocative literary journey, highlighting the struggles and resilience of the impoverished, while exploring the anatomy of love in its myriad forms, a love that sustains and destroys.

—**SUNITA PANT BANSAL**
Mythologist | Decoder of Scriptures | Author of 30 books

Gratitude

A book born to an author is nurtured by a dedicated team. Translating the original work in Malayalam, which narrates the events and lives of the people of erstwhile Travancore, has been a challenging task. I am grateful to Harishna Thampi, a promising young talent, for the assistance rendered. I also express my gratitude to my daughter, Dr Sneha John, who helped me update words and expressions.

I am indebted to my publisher K.P.R. Nair, who, after releasing the original Malayalam work at the Sharjah International Book Fair, sparked the idea of an English version of my novel. I am also thankful to the Konark team, led by the committed Jiza Joy, for their invaluable support.

The captivating illustrations by Prasannan Anickad are what truly bring this book to life. His distinctive cartoon style adds a vibrant, imaginative flair that beautifully enhances the novel. A heartfelt thank you to Prasannan.

Thiruvananthapuram **Prof. Jayalekshmi**

An ululating Kunjikkali

Prologue

A MOTHERLY TOUCH soothed the pangs of birth and rough fingers gently grazed her shoulder, as Ammu felt a shock coursing through her body. A fierce lightning bolt streaked across the sky above the colossal *anjili** tree, followed by a deafening roar of thunder.

Did the lightning strike, or had she stepped on an anjili seed? Ammu stumbled ... But before she fell, a calloused hand gripped her tightly, and a forest-scented breath caressed her nape. An enchanting aroma filled the air.

"*Vaave*,"† an alluring call rang in her ears, and as she flew back on the wings of time, she was once again Ammu Vaava, the cherished little girl. Suddenly, she found herself enmeshed in the dark locks of Kaliamma's hair, reminded of a past she had strayed far from.

"Kaliamma, where were you? I've been searching for you for a long time. I grew exhausted looking for you on Kadankunnu.‡ I roamed around the lake shore, the ezhuthupura§ and even in the heap of ashes in the

---

* A wild jack tree
† An endearing term for a baby/small child
‡ The hill of the foxes
§ An isolated small building detached from the main house, used as a writing space

chambalpura.* Where did you hide? What happened? Tell me ... ," Ammu cried.

"Vaave, release your hold on the *vennil*† vines. You'll cut yourself," came an ethereal voice.

"What! I thought I was holding on to the curly locks of Kaliamma," Ammu exclaimed, loosening her grip from the prickly vennil vines.

"Come with me quickly!" a commanding voice called out from behind. Startled, Ammu looked to see where the voice came from.

A silhouette swayed towards Kadankunnu with the western winds. She didn't need to follow; the winds carried her along.

In a lightning flash, she saw Kaliamma's favourite weapon, the iron *vajrayudham*,‡ or machete, hidden in the thicket. She picked it up from the bush and followed the shadow until she reached a pile of ash. The shadow now appeared to be moving southwest. There, nestled in the dirt, was an uncharred earthen pillar. She nudged the ash-laden pillar with the machete, and in the glow of a firefly, a piece of bone was exposed—a gleaming fragment of an unbent spine. She cradled it with affectionate reverence, holding it close to her bosom and screaming, "Oh, Mother, Oh Kali!"

---

* A shack to collect and preserve leaf ash, which is used as organic fertilizer
† A thorny wild creeper
‡ This is also known as the Hindu god Indra's thunderbolt weapon

The skies screeched and darkness shrouded the lake. "Ammu Vaave, go to the ezhuthupura ... you must start writing!" Kunjikkali called. It was not a hapless cry but an ululation—an intense ululation that reverberated in all eight directions and beyond!

That voice and the clamour slowly faded into nothing. With eyes shedding tears that merged with the raindrops, Ammu watched the dark form take on the colour of the lake, sinking to become a whirlpool in its depths, leaving only bubbles rising to the surface.

Summoning the ethereal force that radiated from the depths of her consciousness, Ammu entered the ezhuthupura, cradling the unbent spine close to her chest. The eternal sacred ancestral lamp atop the mango wood table flickered steadily. Inside the drawer, Ammu discovered an intact ruled notebook from her school days, the one she had used to teach Kunjikkali the alphabet. As she opened it, she saw Kunjikkali's name etched in charcoal on the front page, underlined by the years 1936–1979. *When did you learn to write like this, Kaliamma?* she wondered.

What a silly question! Ammu chided herself. After all, wasn't Kaliamma the one who had taught Ammu about life? Kaliamma, who embodied a textbook in every way. *You are so much more enigmatic than your riddles, my mother!* she realised.

The piercing cry of Kunjikkali, declaring, "I don't need your six feet of earth, nor do I want you to make me a funeral pyre; here goes Kali in a glorious flame", still echoed in Ammu Vaava's ears, breaking her heart.

Resonating from the mother lake, Kunjikkali's ululation reached beyond the four shores of *Pookaithayoor** and into the wider world.

---

* The land of fragrant screw pines

One

AMMU DEVU PILLA was a slender eight-year-old girl, dressed in a mini frock, when Kunjikkali first came into her life. It was also the day Kochuraman married Kunjikkali. Kochuraman, who was the cattle herdsman at *Manthoppu** Bungalow, had just turned twenty. Crippled by polio in his childhood, he was the youngest of the five children of Thevan Thala Pulayan, the chief labourer at Manthoppu. A devastating smallpox outbreak had wiped out Thevan's entire family, who lived in Thekkekara, on the south shore of Pookkaithayoor Lake. Those afflicted, whether alive or dead, were all buried en masse, wrapped in straw mats. When Padmanabha Pilla, the landlord of Manthoppu Bungalow, spotted Thevan's toddler limping out of his hut and crying loudly on the quay, he ordered that the child be brought to the bungalow and be showered, cleaned and fed. He also made arrangements to house the child with Konnan, who looked after the cattle, reprimanding anyone who mocked the lame child.

Kochuraman grew up gulping down freshly squeezed milk early in the morning and eating *pazhamkanji*.† When

---

* Mango grove
† Leftover rice from the previous day mixed with salt, curd, onions, and green chillies

Kochuraman began to cast longing glances at the Dalit Pulaya* women folk working in the paddy fields, *Manthoppilangunnu*† realised that "Kochu"raman was no longer a child, as his name suggested, but had grown into a "Kannali"raman just like the other cattle herders! And so the *Angunnu*‡ asked for the hand of Kunjikkali, daughter of Ayyan of Ambumala, who looked after agriculture at his *Aayirappara Kandam*, a thousand-acre paddy field along the canal's shore, to be Kochuraman's bride.

Ayyan, his wife Kunjola and Kunjikkali's younger brother, Kochucherukkan, were all elated by the proposal and gladly accepted the offer to marry her to Kochuraman. They felt relieved that she wouldn't starve at Manthoppu. Manthoppilangunnu's word was final across Ambumala, where the twelve tenants owned their shelters thanks to the benevolence of his Lordship. He was also known across Pookkaithayoor as *Peshkarangunnu*§ for his altruism, having offered tenancy to landless serfs long before land reform legislation was even conceived.

In contrast to other barons of his stature, Manthoppilangunnu regularly defied prevalent social customs and taboos. He shouldered the responsibilities of his tenants and was actively involved in meeting their needs,

---

* A Dalit sub-caste; a scheduled caste under reservation in the southern states of India
† A term of respect for Padmanabha Pilla, the landlord of Manthoppu Bungalow
‡ Lord/master
§ The title of a revenue officer in Travancore State

from providing shelter and arranging marriages to organising the smooth conduct of their funeral rites. This "Baron of Manthoppu" was a great reformer who was unafraid to challenge the superstitions and outdated customs upheld by both the oppressed and the social elites.

It was highly unusual for barons to personally participate in the betrothals of their tenants. The common practice was for the groom to seek permission to bring the bride to the manor, where the newly-weds would offer money, betel leaves, areca nuts and tobacco to their lord. The baron would then arrive to see the bride and provide the couple with rice, coconuts, cereals, tubers and some money for their living expenses. However, Manthoppilangunnu rejected such customary practices and refused to follow them. For Kochuraman's wedding, he spared no expense; he paid a month in advance 25 bales of paddy and Rs 100 to Ayyan via his steward, Kunjupilla, as the customary bride's price.

"What is this? We are who we are because you have fed us, and now, you expect us to take your money?" Ayyan protested with the utmost humility.

"Your daughter doesn't even need a toe's space to plant paddy saplings in the field. She's precious and worth far more than this money," Manthoppilangunnu retorted. By cancelling the post-wedding feast, he effectively avoided the almost ritualistic disputes and fights that often erupted during and after the banquet. For *Ammutty*,* the day resembled the grand spectacle of the festival of Kasturi Kunnil Bhagothi—

---

* A pet name. Ammutty is a shortened form of *Ammukkutty*; *kutty* is an affectionate suffix used for a child.

the mother goddess of Pookkaithayoor. As she watched the housemaid, Yashodamma, dress Ammu in a new yellow frock and a matching crystal necklace, with her ears adorned with earrings and glass bangles on both hands, Manthoppilamma, her grandmother, playfully teased Ammu, asking if it was her wedding day.

Manthoppilamma disapproved of Manthoppilangunnu and Ammu attending "Kannali" raman's wedding. She grumbled about how these actions defied the family's aristocratic traditions.

In the early morning, Kochuraman bathed in the lake, applied coconut oil to his hair and combed it, and then proceeded to slather his face with the oil, looking even more foolish. Meanwhile, Vasukuttan, the coachman, bathed Manikandan, the bull, and smeared sandal paste on his forehead to make him even more handsome for the occasion. He then adorned the cart with coloured paper streamers.

Ammutty and her *Valiyachan*,* Manthoppilangunnu, climbed onto the plank extended at the back of the wagon and sat on a straw mattress. Vasukuttan, with a *chutti thorthu*† draped over his shoulder, took his place on the seat behind Manikandan. Kochuraman found his spot beside Vasukuttan.

The bells hanging around Manikandan's neck jingled as he pulled the cart, causing the birds to chatter in protest and take flight. Manikandan's brass-covered horns and decorative nose rope added to his regal appearance. No reins or devices were

---

* Maternal grandfather
† A bath towel with dyed corners

necessary to regulate the bull's speed; a simple hum from Vasukuttan was enough to communicate what was needed.

As the party reached the ravine's edge, the ride turned chilly, meandering along the bushy and rocky country roads. Towering bamboo groves, drooping ferns and tiny flowers resembling mustard seeds, along with fleeting glimpses of *manathu kanni*,* which occasionally surfaced only to be immediately clutched by kingfishers diving down from the skies, offered Ammu a series of captivating and novel experiences.

It took them approximately one hour to reach the edge of Aayirappara Kandam, with Ambumala on the opposite side of the canal. The water in the canal was only knee-deep. Manthoppilangunnu folded his milky white khadar dhoti and carefully carried Ammu on his shoulder across the trough, followed by Kochuraman, who struggled to wade through the water. Vasukuttan released Manikandan from the cart and secured him to a bamboo stalk on the canal bank, giving him a reassuring pat on his back and saying, "We'll be back soon, son." On the other side of the canal, the bride's young brother, Kochucherukkan, welcomed the groom by placing a tulsi garland around his neck.

Everyone rinsed their feet with water from a pitcher.

It was nine *vinazhika*† past eight, and the auspicious moment had arrived. Manthoppilangunnu announced, "We

---

* A type of freshwater fish found in Kerala
† A unit of time, 24 seconds

can't delay any longer. We must return to Manthoppu before the sun gets too strong."

The bride's family laid out a white cloth on the plank in the courtyard of their thatched hut. The bride's mother and aunt escorted her to the spot, and the groom and the bride settled into the seats prepared for them on the plank.

In his excitement, Kochuraman had forgotten to unfurl the dhoti he had hastily tied up while crossing the canal. Manthoppilangunnu had to reprimand him for not lowering his dhoti as he sat on the plank. The priest, Velu, then instructed Kochuraman to securely fasten the *thali*[*] around the bride's neck. As Kochuraman attempted to tie the knot with trembling hands, Velu ordered the women folk present to start ululating, a customary expression of joy during the tying of the thali.

Aunt Nangeli and grandmother Kurumbi emitted a noise akin to the howling of dogs, causing a disturbance. Kunjola, the bride's mother, struggled to quell their commotion. Witnessing her mother's predicament, the bride, Kunjikkali, raised her head and let out a tongue-twisting ululation so loud and haunting that it silenced the jarring sounds made by her aunt, mother and grandmother. Her enchanting voice infused such sweetness and harmony, leaving onlookers stunned. "What mischief is this girl up to during her wedding ceremony?!" they exclaimed. However, Manthoppilangunnu appreciated and applauded her sensibility.

---

[*] An auspicious thread knotted around the bride's neck by the groom during a South Indian wedding ceremony

Kunjikkali ululating during her wedding ceremony

Ammutty curiously eyed the bride, whose complexion was the colour of honey. Her eyes were adorned with kohl—a mixture of castor oil, tender betel leaves and lemon juice. Her eyebrows appeared reluctant to meet in the centre. She wore a nose stud resembling a tiny *mukkutti** bloom. Her rosy lips shone brightly, a striking contrast against her ebony face. Palm leaves shaped into hoops dangled from her ears.

Her eyes, like a wild stream with swirling currents yet at times as serene as a lake, conveyed deep emotions through their ever-changing expressions. Her abundant, unruly, curls framed a body as robust as rosewood, drawing attention. Though her smile was tinged with melancholy, her allure remained a mystery. She may not have conformed to conventional standards of beauty, yet there was an inexplicable charm about her—something mystical and otherworldly.

Is she human, or is she Vana Durga, the goddess of the woods? wondered eight-year-old Ammu, utterly captivated.

The *Podava Koda*, the ceremony in which the bridegroom gifts clothes to the bride, marking the final ritual of the wedding, had concluded. Ammutty observed Kunjikkali with a sense of awe and admiration as she hurried into the hut to change her attire, donning the garments presented by the bridegroom. Wearing the muslin dhoti gifted by Kochuraman, Kunjikkali tightened her *rouka*.† Her breasts tamed and demurely covered with a shoulder towel, Kunjikkali emerged from the hut, impressing Manthoppilangunnu with her swiftness.

---

* A tiny perennial herb with immense medicinal benefits
† A mini top worn by women in Kerala in the olden days

When the bride had retreated into the hut to change her clothes, the offerings of beaten rice, betel leaves, areca nuts, tobacco rolls and toddy, all presented as ritual sacrifices to the demigod Madan, were given to the bridegroom's party for consumption. Manthoppilangunnu silently signalled the commencement of the meal. Vasukuttan refreshed himself by chewing tender betel leaves and areca nuts. Meanwhile, Kochuraman was in the process of guzzling from a bottle of toddy, which he reluctantly abandoned upon catching Manthoppilangunnu's furious gaze. Manthoppilangunnu and Ammutty sipped tender coconut water.

The journey back to the bungalow with Kunjikkali was a delightful experience. The scenery they had witnessed from the cart during the onward journey now appeared even more enchanting. The forest seemed to have taken on the mystic charm of Kunjikkali herself. The dark vines resembled her abundant curly locks, hanging from the high branches and dangling in the air. The bluish clouds in the sky appeared to have contoured themselves to match the curves of Kali's form.

The bells hanging around Manikandan jingled like anklets. Meanwhile, Manthoppilangunnu slipped into deep contemplation. With a visible affection for his grandchild, he spoke, "Ammutty, you may sit on your Valiyachan's lap."

This open expression of love was unusual, and it didn't take long for his heart to reveal the reason behind it.

"My dear child, this unlucky father didn't have the opportunity to embark on a journey like this for Devayani's wedding. She was married in the sacred temple of Kasturi Kunnil Bhagothi, just within eyeshot of the western yard of the bungalow. Alas, we did not receive the goddess's blessings, and we lost our daughter prematurely ..."

Manthoppilangunnu paused, his sorrow palpable in a deep sigh. It was at that moment that Ammu felt the gentle touch of Kunjikkali for the first time. Taming her unruly hair caught in the wind, Kali planted a kiss on her forehead. Ammu experienced the soothing coolness of that kiss, followed by a warm embrace from behind, the first of many that would envelop her in sweet sensations. Meanwhile, Kochuraman dozed on Vasukuttan's shoulder, oblivious to it all.

Upon reaching Manthoppu Bungalow, Manthoppilangunnu instructed his steward, Kunjupilla, to ask Manthoppilamma to welcome the bride into the house with a lit lamp. Pilla's room had been temporarily allotted to Kochuraman, and Pilla had been shifted to the room adjacent to the barn.

"Come here, you!" Manthoppilamma called Kunjikkali, her voice devoid of any compassion. Kunjikkali obliged her, showing little concern, and approached the matriarch.

"You, now walk into that eastern room with this lamp facing east. Enter with your right leg first," she ordered. Kunjikkali glanced at the sky, making sure to face the east, and bowed to the sun before entering the room with the lamp.

"Now, you can enter the room," Manthoppilangunnu told Kochuraman. A disinterested Manthoppilamma abandoned the entire charade and headed inside the bungalow. Yashodamma then arrived with a glass of milk and a banana for the newly-weds, following Manthoppilangunnu's instructions.

"This will be your home for some time now. I've arranged a house for Kochuraman in *Thazhethadam*, down the hill. Kunjikkali may move in with her husband once she's familiar with the place and the people here," Manthoppilangunnu said with genuine concern and kindness.

Ammu wanted to ask her grandfather to let Kunjikkali stay at the bungalow. But she decided to save her request for another, opportune moment.

Although Ammu yearned to extend her time with Kunjikkali, she reluctantly headed inside when her grandmother called. That night, as she lay alone on her bed in the *kizhakkini** room, Ammu sensed a presence at Manthoppu as pure and gentle as the moonlight caressing her.

---

* The eastern block of a house

Two

AMMUTTY AWOKE TO the sound of a folk ballad the following day.

"*Ramante Seethe terekkettumbam ente cheethe cherekkettum* (രാമന്റെ സീതേ തേരേക്കേറ്റുമ്പം ഏനെന്റെ ചീതേ ചേരേക്കേറ്റും)" meaning when Lord Sree Rama lifts his wife Seetha to the chariot, I will lift my Cheetha* to the wall.

Through her open window, she watched as Kunjikkali swept the courtyard. There was a touch of wistful humour on her face, yet her cheeks shone red with the tender kisses of the morning sun. She looked up and called out to Ammutty with great affection. "Come on over here ..."

Ammu descended to the courtyard, washed her face with a handful of fresh, cool water drawn from the well by Kali, brushed her teeth with *umikkari*† and then went to her Valiyachan for her customary share of his *karupatti kaapi*‡ mixed with ghee. That day, the idea of going to school didn't appeal to her. She longed to wander the mango grove with Kunjikkali. However, she remained silent, fearful of her grandmother's disapproval. Instead, she ran to the lake for

---

* A name resembling Seetha that is commonly used by Dalits
† Burnt paddy husk used for cleaning teeth
‡ Black coffee sweetened with palm jaggery

Ammu watching Kunjikkali sweeping the yard

a quick dip, determined to reach it before her Valiyachan returned from his morning yoga and bath. Kunjikkali joined her without a need for Ammu to ask, and they went down the Kadankunnu together. "I shall stay here until Angunnu finishes his bath. Vaava may join him," Kunjikkali said.

"Vaava", a mother's endearing call to a child, the first of its kind, stirred something deep within Ammu. The child in her yearned to be cuddled and embraced. Meanwhile, Kunjikkali got busy collecting all the midribs scattered under the coconut trees without wasting any time. Ammu eagerly leaped into the lake, informing her Valiyachan that Kunjikkali had accompanied her. "In that case, let her come here and enjoy the lake while keeping Ammutty company," Manthoppilangunnu said before departing. Kunjikkali, now at the lakeside, waded knee-deep into the water. She turned eastwards, bowed to the rising sun with joined palms, and then submerged herself in the lake. Ammu was startled to see Kali vanish beneath the water's surface. However, within a few moments, she reappeared nearby. It was the first time Ammu had witnessed this trick of hiding beneath the ripples and then emerging. "It's called *mungaamkuzhi* ... Vaava can also perform this trick. Kaliamma will teach you."

"Kali Amma." "Amma ..." Ammutty loved the very word. Kaliamma gently scrubbed Ammu with a loofah, lovingly bathed her and towel-dried her hair, just as mothers do. When she bathed alone, Ammu would never take her clothes off and disrobe entirely. She would then dash to the bungalow completely soaked, and her hurried run would partially dry her along the way. But now, for the first time, Ammu experienced the joys of a child being cared for by its mother.

When the children playing in the mango grove caught sight of the radiant little Ammu, her hair neatly combed and braided with jasmine on either side, her eyes accentuated by eyeliner, and her forehead adorned with red kumkumam and sandalwood paste, they erupted in ecstasy, exclaiming, "Princess!"

Thus, Ammu Devu Pilla of Manthoppu Bungalow transformed into the princess who led the battalion of children marching to Achyutha Vilasam School. That day, Ammu decided not to spend her after-school hours with her friends, wandering along the lake shore, playing in the water, flinging stones into the lake and drenching each other in playful splashes.

She had promised to give Kunjikkali a tour around the mango grove. And so, upon returning from school, she changed her clothes, took a bite of the special unbreakable *Kaliodakka*,* a Yashodamma speciality, and then embarked on her adventure with Kunjikkali.

Pookkaithayoor was a village defined by its simple elegance. At its heart lay an expansive body of water, known to some as *vaanarakkulam*, or monkey pond. One legend tells of a thirsty Hanuman, who, on his journey to meet Sita in Lanka when she was imprisoned by Ravana, reached the valley and dug this pond with his tail. For others, it was called *kidaathikulam*, filled with the tears of Neelippennu, an adolescent Dalit girl. Unaware that her lover Samban had been attacked by a leopard on his pilgrimage to Sabarimala,

---

* A traditional Kerala snack made of rice flour

she endlessly awaited his return in the valley. When she eventually learned of his demise, she tragically ended her life in the same lake. Local folklore sang ballads of her ghost haunting the lake. The elders of the four hills surrounding the lake worshipped it as a sacred virgin with no inlets or outlets. They would commence their day only after paying their respects to this mother lake. Grannies would sing fairy tales of Neelippennu enticing daring youngsters who gazed too long into the depths of the unfathomable waters. And as if to preserve the innocence of this virgin mother lake, a natural fence of *Pookkaitha* plants formed on all sides. Clustered together and rooted in sand and mud, these *kaitha* plants sealed off both entries and exits. The female screw pines leaned and gracefully arched as they grew, while the male pines grew straight towards the skies, blossoming every *Chingam*, the first month of the Malayalam calendar. They added a delightful fragrance to the land, particularly during Onam, the harvest festival.

Three

THE MANTHOPPU BUNGALOW proved to be a breathtaking spectacle for the people of Pookkaithayoor. Under the watchful eye of the chief carpenter, Velu Asari, a dedicated team of temple builders from Nagercoil took two years to craft this architectural marvel. This splendid structure boasted a capacious prayer room that could comfortably house the entire pantheon of Hindu deities. The traditional *naalukettu's** imposing facades, accompanied by a vault, granary, barn, and its cardinal-facing wings, were a testament to its grandeur. The bungalow consisted of numerous rooms, vast galleries, lengthy patios and a porch adorned with intricate carvings, including a captivating lotus in full bloom.

Inside, the imposing teakwood dining table could effortlessly accommodate twenty guests. The granary was brimming with an abundance of paddy and the cavernous cellar was filled with boiled rice, while unhusked rice was stored in a massive wooden box placed on the extensive east-facing kitchen platform. The cellar also held large quantities of bananas, varieties of small plantains, vegetables and pulses.

---

* A traditional Kerala house with a rectangular structure where four blocks—east, west, north, and south—are connected by an open courtyard

Adjacent to the cellar lay the spacious twenty-foot kitchen, with its northern vestibule housing essential tools such as the grindstone, millstone, pestle and mortar. Outside the kitchen was a firewood shack for fuelling the cooking fires.

The bungalow boasted two toilets, one in the west and the other in the south, both outside the main building. In front of the bungalow, was a thatched, sloping long shed with a bench, desk and plantain leaves, ensuring food for any hungry person who happened to come along. It was Manthoppilangunnu's mandate to always serve food to the needy. Every night at supper time, caretaker Kunjan Pillai would stand at the entrance of Manthoppu, calling out asking if there was anyone who hadn't eaten. Atop the table, a large copper pot always held *jeeraka*[*] water, and plantain stalks hung, much like in local fruit shops, for the benefit of all.

The large well in the northeastern corner of the property was a perennial source of pure drinking water, plunging a remarkable twenty-eight fathoms deep. The water possessed the fragrant essence reminiscent of the healing properties of *neelakoduveli*.[†] At the bottom of the well rested the *nellippalaka*—a wooden ring crafted from gooseberry wood that added an earthy sweetness to the water. Pointing south to north was the cattle shed, which provided shelter to the cows and calves.

The two cattle herds, Konnan and Kochuraman, lived in the room adjacent to the cattle shed. The oxen were kept in the big cattle shed near the Aayirappara Kandam, where they

---

[*] Cumin seeds
[†] An indigenous medicinal herb

were looked after by Ayyan, the head labourer. Manikandan, the ox that pulled the bullock carriage, was housed in a well-kept shed to the south, and Vasukkuttan, the bullock driver, lived in the room attached to the shed. The housekeeper, Yashodamma, and the housemaid, Daivathaal, were accommodated in the servants' room close to the kitchen.

The Manthoppu Bungalow exuded prosperity and contentment from every angle. However, even more remarkable than the bungalow itself was the living legend, Manthoppilangunnu, also widely known as Peshkarangunnu. He held the prestigious position of a writer at the *hajur kacheri*, or secretariat in Thiruvananthapuram (earlier known as Trivandrum), the capital of Kerala. His official duties included issuing royal orders, proclamations and the safekeeping of official records. This role was considered immensely influential; hence, Padmanabha Pilla earned the title of Peshkarangunnu among the people of Pookkaithayoor, a blessed land graced by hillocks, lakes, fresh air and pure water.

Even before the construction of the bungalow, Peshkarangunnu enriched the land by planting an array of mango trees, coconut trees and various other fruits. His vision was to have his house nestled within a thriving mango grove, and he planted a diverse range of mango trees. The bungalow's surroundings were adorned with *muvandan, kilichundan, naattumaanga, shoorankudi, kappamaanga, ottumaanga,* the exotic *malgoa, neelam, alfonso* and numerous other unknown mango varieties. Peshkarangunnu firmly believed that mango trees infused the air with pure oxygen.

These fruits were intended not only for the household but also for all the children, birds and animals in the vicinity.

While Padmanabha Pilla was away at work, his wife Rudrani Thankachi, and their infant son and youngest of three children, Madhavan, moved into the Manthoppu Bungalow. She fancied herself the matriarch and believed, *I am the monarch of all I survey*. She was obsessed with acquiring properties and wealth while severely lacking in human compassion.

As Pookkaithayoor lacked educational institutions during that era, Sivasuthan, the firstborn son, and Devayani, the daughter of Padmanabhan and Rudrani Thankachi, resided with their father in Vellayambalam, Thiruvananthapuram, to pursue their studies.

Even upon his return to Manthoppu after retiring from government service, he remained the revered Peshkarangunnu for the villagers. They respected and obeyed him; he was both their protector and dispenser of justice. In his eyes, every fellow human was equal, and he showered mercy on the vulnerable but none when punishing wrongdoers. A popular legend in the village prevailed about him being so strong that a single slap from his right hand could knock anyone down; hence, he only used his left hand! He treated both men and women with impartiality but did not hesitate to reprimand or even punish them when they overstepped boundaries. He had great affection for children, and his instructions were always infused with love. He was keenly interested in the common good and had his pulse on the Renaissance movement in Kerala. And he was extremely handsome too; he had a tall, well-built frame, arresting eyes, a sharp nose, a broad forehead and a fair complexion.

Early in the morning, he would stroll through the hillock wearing nothing but a loincloth, making his way to the serene lakeside. Upon reaching, he would hang his workout rings on the wormwood branches and perform his exercise routine on the sand bed before moving on to his yoga practice. One particular day, one of Thevan's children was startled when he chanced upon Peshkarangunnu hanging upside down while executing the complex *shirshasana*, or headstand. The terrified child cried out for help and ran until he reached the bungalow, collapsing out of breath. Even today, the workers at Manthoppu share a hearty laugh at the expense of the innocent boy.

Following his rigorous workouts, he would descend to the lake and swim elegant backstrokes and breaststrokes. Occasionally, he would simply lie still, floating on the tranquil waters. After a refreshing bath at the lake, he would return to the bungalow for his breakfast of *puttu*, a steamed cake made of unhusked and unboiled rice, mashed with a small yellow banana and some honey. He abstained from tea and coffee, preferring only lukewarm water. After breakfast, he would rest in his armchair for half an hour and then proceed to the southern verandah to spin the *charkha*.* Every piece of clothing he used, including his loincloth, was made from pure khadi. He followed a strict routine and was very meticulous and punctual. He had his lunch at exactly 1 p.m. every day, and it was always the same: boiled rice, curd,

---

* A wheel used to spin yarn

aviyal* and a vegetable stir fry made with bitter gourd, okra and snake gourd. His dinner consisted of broken brown rice porridge, green gram and roasted *pappadam*. Before retiring for the night, he always drank a cup of fresh cow milk. He was a strict vegetarian.

Kayalamma Motors, the only bus service to Bhagothimukku, the junction near the temple, arrived daily at noon, delivering the *Malayala Rajyam* newspaper. It was Kochuraman's job to fetch the newspaper from Pattukada Viswambharan's provision store. Peshkarangunnu would quickly glance through it but would wait for Ammu to read it aloud. After enjoying *idiyappam, therali* or *pazhampori* (popular snacks in Kerala) on her return from school, Ammu was expected to take her seat on the stool next to her Valiyachan. He himself would be comfortably settled in his armchair beneath the shade of the mango tree. The workers were expected to finish their tasks, shower and assemble on the verandah of the cattle shed at 5 p.m. sharp.

Once he was sure everyone was in their seats, Peshkarangunnu would ask Ammu to begin reading. He would say, "Ammutty, you may start reading now. Read aloud from page one to the last, and be sure to pronounce words such as *bharatham, dharmam,* etc., correctly." If Ammu fumbled or made a mistake, Peshkarangunnu would correct her. In the midst of her reading, he would offer explanations and comments on the news. Sometimes there would be questions as well. However, not a single day would pass without Peshkarangunnu speaking about Mahatma Gandhi; he was a devout disciple of Gandhiji.

---

* A mixed vegetable dish

Peshkarangunnu glancing over the newspaper

Following the newspaper reading session, Peshkarangunnu would elaborate on the major tasks for the next day and assign duties to everyone. Angunnu was also open to suggestions from the workers, reflecting his commitment to discipline and teamwork.

Peshkarangunnu always remained true to his word, and the doors of his abode remained open to all. Anyone was welcome to draw water from his well or utilise his kitchen facilities for cooking and feasting.

However, all of Peshkarangunnu's actions deeply unsettled those who considered themselves *savarna** and tried in vain to correct him by reiterating all the customs and taboos. He further disappointed the local elites, who had aspirations of marrying off their sons or nephews to his daughter Devayani. Peshkarangunnu disappointed all of them by strictly adhering to his principles and convictions, forcing them to ditch their plans for a Manthoppu alliance. It was inconceivable for them to associate with a family that did not prioritize their caste traditions, regardless of their wealth. However, Peshkarangunnu remained unfazed and proceeded to find a suitable groom from the most southern district for his daughter, marrying her off with great pomp and glory.

Pookkaithayoor was rife with fanciful stories of Peshkarangunnu's inhuman strength and fearlessness. One such tale revolved around the Thulukkan band of robbers, notorious for mugging and robbing travellers who disembarked from the bus at Bhagothimukku en route to the

---

* High caste

lake. One day, Peshkarangunnu took that very road disguised as a woman bedecked in all her glistening gold. Before the bandit could disorient him with a sack, Peshkarangunnu caught him and delivered a thorough thrashing. The rest of the gang received a good taste of his whip as they fled for their lives. One unfortunate gang member was struck down by Peshkarangunnu's right palm and tumbled into the canal, regaining consciousness only on the third day. Peshkarangunnu was unquestionably the de facto police and magistrate of Pookkaithayoor.

Four

MANTHOPPILAMMA STOOD IN stark contrast to Padmanabha Pilla. She exuded ostentation, reserving the title *Amma* (mother) exclusively for her children, while insisting that all servants address her formally as *Thambratti* (my lady). Her neck was adorned with necklaces and medallions, and her ears sparkled with seven-stone-studded earrings. Intricate nose studs embellished her nose, and she wore shiny gold bangles, a gold-embroidered dhoti and upper cloth—all contributing to her unmistakable air of nobility. This aristocratic aura extended beyond her attire to her demeanour. Whether issuing commands from the swinging bed in the *idappura*, the central room in the house, or from the sofa on the western verandah, she asserted her authority with unwavering confidence.

In her view, all servants were nothing more than subservient slaves, and she personified the rigid social hierarchies of the time. She showed no tolerance for individuals from lower castes entering the bungalow or working in the kitchen, openly opposing the progressive reforms advocated by Padmanabha Pilla.

Rudrani Thankachi aka *Manthoppilamma*

Ammu observed the contrasting personalities of Valiyachan and *Ammamma** on the very day Kunjikkali was brought to their home. Valiyachan welcomed her with affection, treating her like a daughter, whereas Ammamma appeared more focused on asserting her authority over the new maid. She exuded the pride of her titled lineage, embodying a mix of authority, beauty, and extravagance. She viewed everything and everyone as her possessions, including her husband and son, whom she expected to obey her commands and fulfil her desires promptly without question. It was evident that she had no love for anyone but herself.

Rudrani Thankachi belonged to the prestigious Karthiyayini Thankachi lineage of Koyikkal Kovilakam, a noble family honoured with titles and expansive, tax-free lands by the Travancore royal family. However, their family fortunes took a downturn due to protracted legal battles and disputes over property rights among family members. They adopted the perspective that "a cowshed cannot shelter an elephant, even if it has shrunk". This attitude was prevalent within the family, particularly among the women, who found it difficult to adjust to their changed circumstances. They remained bitter, arrogant and demanding.

Thus, Rudrani Thankachi reigned as the unofficial queen in a fool's paradise. She held sway over Manthoppu while Padmanabha Pilla worked in Thiruvananthapuram. Even upon his retirement, she showed no inclination to relinquish her self-appointed throne. Her husband, who was primarily

---

* Grandmother

engrossed in the public affairs of the village anyway, never bothered to get involved in her governance.

Rudrani Thankachi assumed a position as if she were the sovereign of the land, consistently ensuring her luxurious preferences took precedence, often sidelining the needs of her husband and children. She seemed immovable in her ways. Every morning, her routine included an hour-long oil bath. She lavishly applied *neelibhringadi*, an expensive Ayurvedic hair-growth oil, on her head, followed by *pindathailam*, a cool moisturiser, on her entire body, and waited for half an hour before bathing. After her bath, she indulged in a sumptuous porridge breakfast. Every year, an entire month was dedicated to her rejuvenating treatments.

Vadakkunthala Thanki *Aasatti*,[*] a renowned masseuse, took residence in the bungalow for this entire month. The aasatti, who wore a thick, broad dhothi, had her breasts hanging sideways in a girdle. She had the complexion of the dark oil that she applied and its fragrance permeated her presence. Inside the *nalukettu*, a copper vessel brimmed with *dhanwantharam* oil, intended for healing bodily wear and tear. The pindathailam, simmered to a rich, blood-red hue in a round *uruli* made of bell metal, preserved youthful skin. To prepare the *thailam*, the children were entrusted with collecting *thechipoovu*.[†] They ventured along the forest path adjacent to the canal leading to the lake, with areca palm spathes in tow. Kovalan and Kuttan would lead the way by pulling the spathe, playfully teasing each other over their

---

[*] Expert masseuse
[†] West Indian jasmine

torn khaki trousers and exposed buttocks. The darkest *thechi* plants thrived along the lakeshore.

Delighted by the freshly picked flowers, Manthoppilamma would distribute ten *narangamittai** into the eager little hands of the children. She would then summon Ammutty from the *arappura*† and offer her a portion of the sweet along with an *unniyappam*‡ from the Ganapati temple, instructing her to enjoy it right away because there wasn't enough for the rest of the children.

Rudrani Thankachi's cunning nature became apparent on many such occasions. She was the type of Ammamma who displayed affection solely when it served her purpose. This trait extended even to her children. She estranged her eldest son, who had been beloved until then, simply because he wanted to marry the girl he loved. This son, who had been sending most of his salary to her, keeping only a small amount for himself, suddenly became estranged. When her husband prepared to leave for Bombay to fulfil their son's wish, she vehemently opposed it, going to extreme lengths by locking herself inside the cellar for seven days without food or water. She only relented and opened the door when Padmanabhan promised her that he wouldn't proceed to Bombay.

She loved her youngest son, Madhavan Pilla, the most and didn't want him to marry because she didn't want to

---

* Tiny orange-flavoured sweets
† Granary
‡ Sweet rice fritters; also a main offering at Ganapati temples in Kerala

share him with anyone else. Being a wily fox himself, this favourite son of hers declared his disdain for anything that his mother disapproved of. Kittan Jolsyar, the astrologer, regularly visited the bungalow to provide his monthly predictions. With a single glance at the horoscope of a prospective bride, he would reveal a lack of "divine pleasure". Aware of Manthoppilamma's innermost desires, Kittan consistently unearthed various bad omens and flaws within the girl and her horoscope.

The servants and villagers had long been perplexed by the mighty Peshkarangunnu's tolerance for his wife's arrogance. There was a secret burning in his heart that no one knew about. It was the story of Padmanabhan, the son of Sekhara Pilla, a humble merchant from the handloom village of Balaramapuram, and his profound obligation to his guru, Achyuthan Pillai.

During Maharaja Balarama Varma's reign in Travancore, Dewan Ummini Thampy orchestrated the relocation of seven families from Nagercoil, hailing from the Shalya community. These seven families were responsible for weaving fabrics exclusively for the royal palace. Thus, the village where these weavers settled acquired the name Balaramapuram. Padmanabha Pilla was entrusted with the job of delivering woven fabrics to the palace in the capital city. However, what appealed most to young Padmanabhan was neither the Kowdiar Palace nor Kanakakunnu but rather His Highness Maharaja's College in the capital city. He would fix his gaze upon that architectural marvel built in the Victorian style and envision the vast reservoir of knowledge that lay within those hallowed halls.

When the brilliant Padmanabhan expressed his aspiration for further education after school, Sekhara Pilla did not oppose him. The mathematics professor, Achyuthan Pillai, noticed the sweaty student, who walked twenty kilometres from Balaramapuram to the college in the city and was always late to his class. Soon, he discovered this diligent student's passion for learning. One day, he extended an invitation to Padmanabhan to live in his home and continue with his studies. Rudrani Thankachi was Achyuthan Pillai's only daughter, and he adored her. Having lost her mother at the age of eight, she was raised by Achyuthan Pillai with the love and care of both a father and a mother. Consequently, he had never lifted a finger at her, adding to her growing sense of false pride and arrogance. She despised Padmanabhan and vehemently opposed the idea of accommodating the poor boy in their home.

Achyuthan Pillai, renowned for his mathematics instruction to the royal prince, had earned the favour of the Dewan. Upon Padmanabhan's completion of his BA (with honours) from Madras University, Achyuthan Pillai secured him a position as a writer in the Hajur Kacheri. Subsequent promotions were solely the result of Padmanabhan's merit and integrity.

Meanwhile, Achyuthan Pillai's life was being gradually claimed by tuberculosis and a chronic cough. His condition further deteriorated during the typhoid epidemic, with no available cure for the illness at that time. He narrowly escaped its clutches, but there was little left to his name except his well-regarded reputation. His chief concern now centred on his only daughter, Rudrani.

Padmanabhan's appointment in the capital city came as a relief for Achyuthan Pillai, who had always regarded him as a son. When Padmanabhan requested permission to move out into a rented house at Vazhuthacaud, near his office, the bedridden teacher expressed his desire to see his daughter married to his protégé. Padmanabha Pilla willingly agreed, as he saw this as a way to repay and honour his teacher. And that was how Padmanabha Pilla married Rudrani Thankachi. Achyuthan Pillai passed away a few days after the wedding. Even in his final moments, he sought assurance in the eyes of his loyal disciple that his only daughter would be loved and protected.

Padmanabhan honoured the memory of his teacher by loving and respecting his daughter and never opposing her in any matter. He considered himself deeply indebted to her father and willingly committed his life to serving and repaying that debt by safeguarding and cherishing his wife.

Five

AMMUTTY AND KUNJIKKALI, lost in their stories and explorations, were completely unaware of the time slipping away. They hurried back to the bungalow as the western sky darkened, tinged with a reddish hue. "Is Kalippennu wandering around the village at the time of twilight prayers? Have you decided to expose this orphan child to the risk of catching a fever?" Ammamma mercilessly yelled at Kunjikkali. A startled Ammu was on the verge of bursting into tears. But when she glanced at Kaliyamma's face, she just stood stoic and unbothered.

That night, Ammu found herself lost in thoughts about her parents. Her mother, Devayani, carried with her the sweet scent of *kaithapoo*.* Every night, Ammu fell asleep to the scent of her mother's saree. This same fragrance filled the room whenever she opened the wardrobe. In her bedroom, a framed wedding photo of her parents hung on the wall—her mother with moist eyes and a pleasant face, and her father with straight hair and a dark moustache. Recollections of fleeting moments from the past lingered in Ammu's mind—the tender touch at night, like a distant dream; the echoes of

---

* Pandanus; extremely fragrant flowers with thorns, and used to grow along the riverbanks in Kerala

the lullaby '*Omanathinkalkidavo*' from a time long gone; the taste of sweets on her tongue on her second birthday. During lonely nights, she was haunted by the memory of the night before her mother's departure—of her embrace and kisses mixed with salty tears as she sobbed and said, "Amma's own darling Ammu."

When Ammu woke up in the morning, her mother was not in her bed. "*What happened?*" she wondered all day. Finally, she decided to ask her grandfather, who was in the middle of his post-dinner meditation on the southern verandah. Ammu often wondered if Valiyachan was praying to Kaayalamma, Mother Lake. Careful not to disturb him, Ammu seated herself on the floor near Valiyachan's wicker chair. "What's on your mind, Ammutty?" he enquired, opening his eyes. "Won't my parents come back, Valiyacha? You said they would be back by the summer vacation, but Ammamma says I do not have a mother or father anymore!" Ammutty burst into tears. "Do not cry, my child; come, sit on Valiyachan's lap, I'll tell you," he said, lifting her onto his lap and continuing.

"Devayani was a sweetheart, just like you, Ammutty. She was pure gold, like a goddess. In those days, Pookkaithayoor did not have any educational institutions. So, my two older children lived with me in Thiruvananthapuram to pursue their studies. The brother and sister were deeply attached to each other. They were good at their studies, too. They would come to Manthoppu during their vacations. Sivasuthan completed his studies at University College, and Devayani at Women's College. Higher education flourished with the establishment of the Travancore University by

His Highness Chithira Thirunal. Sivan proceeded with his master's in chemistry, but Devayani was interested in mathematics, just like me. She was a voracious reader. For every vacation, she would carry a load of books from the university library to Pookkaithayoor. Her reading included the works of freedom fighters such as Mahatma Gandhi, Jawaharlal Nehru, Subhas Chandra Bose, Sardar Vallabhbhai Patel and so on.

"The Temple Entry Proclamation of 1936 by Sree Chithira Tirunal Balarama Varma opened the temples to all Hindus, irrespective of their caste. Gandhiji praised the Maharaja by calling him a *"Mahatma"*. Before that, in 1920, Gandhiji visited the Chattampi Swamikal Memorial at Panmana Ashram. The enlightened leader of Travancore, Kumbalath Sankupilla, received Gandhiji and organised an interaction with the public. I was an honours student then and went to Panmana Ashram to meet the Mahatma. Gandhiji's speech that day touched many hearts. He asked the women folk gathered there, 'Aren't you ashamed of wearing all these gold ornaments while the destitute Harijans starve? I address you today with a plea to feed them.' The women who felt their conscience prick them pledged their gold to Gandhiji. When I narrated this incident to Devayani, she listened ardently and immediately removed her gold earrings, chain and bangles, and pledged, 'This gold will go to Bapuji's fund. I will give it to him the next time he visits.'

"Gandhiji visited Thiruvananthapuram in 1937 and participated in the Temple Entry Proclamation celebrations. He then visited Ayyankali, the fighter of the oppressed

Devayani handing over her gold ornaments to Mahatma Gandhi

Dalits, at Venganoor and established a warm relationship with him. I went along with Devayani to meet Gandhiji. She prostrated before him, surrendered her jewellery and vowed never to wear gold again. When we returned, having sought the blessings of Gandhiji, I was proud of my daughter and her benevolence. But her mother was furious upon hearing this story. 'Now that you've decided you don't need any gold, you won't receive any from this house for your marriage. All the jewellery—the *mullamottu mala** *adyal*† and gold bangles—none of it belongs to you anymore. I will give it all to Madhavan's wife.' 'As you wish, Amma. All I need is this pearl necklace, glass bangles and these stone earrings,' Devayani retorted.

"I did not take this bickering between the mother and the daughter seriously. However, Devayani stood her ground, even at her wedding. She did not budge from her decision at all. The family of Parameswara Pilla arrived with all the grandeur of the Neyyattinkara Nairs in motor cars never seen in Pookkaithayoor before. The decorations and attire were a novel sight in the village. A magnificent canopy decorated with palm leaves arose in the courtyard of Manthoppu Bungalow for the wedding. A boat loaded with everything necessary for the grand wedding feast docked at the river and was transported from there to the bungalow on bullock carts. The *nadaswarammelam*‡ began, and Devayani Pilla, the bride,

---

* Jasmine bud-shaped gold necklace
† A necklace studded with precious stones
‡ Orchestra of traditional instruments

appeared radiant as a goddess. All those present to witness her beauty joined their palms in reverence. To everyone's surprise, the only ornaments she wore were stone earrings, a white pearl necklace and black glass bangles. 'Why is she dressed like this? Doesn't the bride of Manthoppu Bungalow have any gold for her marriage?!' people exclaimed. 'Such insolence!' Ammamma grumbled. Meanwhile, Daivatthaal, who had lulled Devayani to sleep from her early childhood, hummed, *'Ponnum kudathinu pottu venda'*, meaning a pot of gold does not require any embellishments.

"Devu wished to find a job and settle down in Thiruvananthapuram. But as I was approaching retirement, I yearned to see my daughter's marriage before it became too late for me. Sadly, they were only together for three and a half years. And they left, leaving me with my precious Ammutty," Valiyachan wept.

"Your father, Parameswara Pilla, was interested in business. When he married Devayani, he was running a wholesale rice business in the Chala market in Thiruvananthapuram. In those days, the South African city of Durban attracted many Indian merchants. Parameswaran, too, expressed great interest in that trade. Devayani was six months pregnant at the time, so she couldn't join him. Parameswaran returned from Durban after three years. He travelled between our bungalow and his family home for a month.

"As his business was flourishing, he needed help with tallying the bills. How could I refuse when he expressed his desire to take Devayani with him? You were just a small child then, too young to be taken abroad. So I suggested that you stay with me for the time being. A month after their departure from here, riots broke out in Durban."

Valiyachan was referring to the Durban riots of 1949. "The Zulus of South Africa looted the shops owned by Indians in Durban. Buildings were set ablaze, and 141 people were burned alive or slaughtered. We heard reports of British women celebrating these killings, dancing with the Zulus, revelling in the deaths of 'Indian Coolies'. Perhaps they were vengeful towards a newly independent India. When the riots finally ended after three days of carnage, my daughter and her husband were among the dead. The authorities remained silent. No one spoke out against this mass murder and appalling racial discrimination."

Valiyachan seethed with anger as he continued, "The world learnt of this tragedy only later, and because it occurred on a distant continent, reaching there was no easy task. We ousted those foreign rulers who wielded power by trampling on the blood of humans, stirring up hatred, division, and chaos among people. Mahatmaji's paths of *ahimsa* and non-cooperation succeeded. We won our freedom, not through arms, but through the strength of our spirits. We must be self-reliant in earning our livelihood, clothing, and shelter. We must never again submit to anyone."

After he expressed his convictions, Ammu finally understood why Valiyachan spun his charkha every day and wore homespun khadi. "We must uplift the weaker among us through education. For the next academic year, we must enrol all the children in our village at Achyutha Vilasam School. Now go to bed, my dear child."

Sleep eluded Ammu that night. She reached beneath the cot, retrieved her mother's box, and took out her mother's saree, which carried the fragrance of kaithapoo. Wrapping herself in it, she sought comfort in its warmth and eventually drifted off to sleep close to midnight. However, a vivid and unsettling dream interrupted her sleep. In it, she felt a searing fire consuming her, and in her fright, she cried out, "Oh Mother! Fire!" Her panicked scream echoed through the entire bungalow, rousing everyone from their slumber. Yashodamma, who slept in the adjacent small room, and Ammamma in the middle chamber, rushed to Ammutty's side. Hearing the commotion and seeing lights turn on inside, Kunjikkali hurried into the bungalow through the half door in the east.

"Give the kid some water to drink, Yashodamma. Shouldn't she be inside for her twilight prayers instead of wandering the woods with the bride? It's the hour when spirits and ghosts wander, and she must have seen something to be so terrified," Ammamma said, casting a sharp glance at Kunjikkali before returning to her room to resume her sleep.

Ammu found solace in knowing that Valiyachan, sleeping in the southern room, remained undisturbed by the commotion. Everyone else went back to sleep except Kunjikkali, who stayed back, holding Ammutty close and comforting her. Eventually, she gently settled into bed with Ammu.

"My dearest child, sleep now. Whether fire or water, nothing will harm you, for Kaliamma is here with you. *Vaave vaave, urangu vaave... kunju vaave, kali vaave...* (Sleep baby sleep, sleep little one, Kali's babe)" she sang. It was as soothing as a lullaby, offering solace to Ammu, who peacefully fell asleep in Kunjikkali's embrace.

Six

PESHKARANGUNNU'S COMMITMENT TO uplift and educate the oppressed was, indeed, a firm decision and the very raison d'être of the Achyutha Vilasam School. Situated on an expansive five-acre plot atop the *kizhakkekkunnu*, an eastern hillock parallel to the kadankunnu, the school was surrounded by *varikka chakka* (a variety of jackfruit) and a few *koozha chakka* (the softer variety of jackfruit) trees, which yielded abundant fruits as though in a frenzy. The coconut trees, too, bore plentiful fruits.

At the centre of the plot was a thatched, long shed made of bamboo and reed. The tiled roof of the office was supported by beams fashioned out of coconut timber, and to the south were the toilets—unusual in those days. This was the beginning of the Achyutha Vilasam School. Every single child of Pookkaithayoor was accepted into the school, irrespective of caste or creed. They travelled by canoe or on foot from the four flanks of the lake. The public road was adjacent to Vadakkekara, which was on Manthoppu Bungalow's north hillside. When students from the Padinjarekkara western shore arrived at the bungalow, they were welcomed with breakfast and seasonal fruits waiting for them on a desk in the courtyard. The children could eat to their hearts' content, and they were free to pelt stones at mangoes if that's what they felt like doing instead.

However, Kochuraman had never been fond of children and their playfulness. One reason was that they often teased him by calling him *Njondi* Raman (lame Raman). Once, noticing a red cloth tied to a branch of the mango tree, Peshkarangunnu enquired, "What is this flag atop the mango tree in the morning?" When he received no response, he summoned his steward, Kunjupilla, who came with utmost humility and informed him that the flag was Kochuraman's handiwork.

"Bring him here," Peshkarangunnu ordered.

Kochuraman appeared, and when asked about the red cloth, he stuttered, "It was an offering to Parankimala Appooppan."

"For what?" Peshkarangunnu asked.

"To prevent those schoolchildren from throwing stones and fronds at the mango tree. Once, they even fell on my leg, causing injury. But those children fled, mocking me as lame."

"But why do you stand under the mango tree? Remove that flag," Peshkarangunnu commanded. "Kochuraman, which *appooppan** is ever angry over kids plucking mangoes? Instead, wouldn't loving grandfathers be furious at those who deny mangoes to children? The mango tree itself would disapprove and stop bearing fruits."

Reluctantly, Kochuraman climbed the tree, removed the flag, and stood in silence.

---

* Grandfather

"The mango tree blooms and bears fruits not only for us but also for these children." Grumbling that he would never understand Angunnu, who was beyond redemption, Kochuraman shot a furious glance at Kunjikkali and stormed into the cowshed.

Peshkarangunnu employed all the tactics of *saamam* (conciliation), *daanam* (gift), *bhedam* (questioning) and *dandam* (punishment) to correct Kochuraman. Manthopillamma despised him, viewing him as useless and fit only to be a pillar of the *thekkepura*, or southern porch. Once, she thrashed him with a bamboo stick for spilling a vessel full of fresh milk, intensifying his hatred towards her. However, Peshkarangunnu, compassionate as ever, didn't have the heart to abandon this orphan boy. He was hopeful that a good woman could transform him.

Every day, after consuming a pot of rice gruel, Kochuraman would climb the kadankunnu to graze the cattle. However, when the parched cattle returned to their shed at the bungalow, Kochuraman was nowhere to be found. He would be sleeping under a cashew tree. Kunjikkali knew about Gomathi cow's dislike to her husband. Gomathi would kick him when his rough, loveless hands tried to milk her. Kunjikkali would then go to her and whisper that she, too, wanted to kick him hard! She would then gently stroke Gomathi's back and wash her udder, causing it yield milk abundantly.

Sadly, Kali's resourcefulness and intelligence failed to evoke any soft feelings in Kochuraman; they only exacerbated his inferiority complex. He was a womaniser, and even marriage did not change that. He enjoyed wooing and flirting

Kochuraman grazing the cattle

with other women who worked with him and watching women bathe in the lake. He was oblivious to the concept of love and engaged in physical intimacy without seeking pleasure. For him, it was a cruel game of causing pain to his partner.

At dawn, Kunjikkali's broom danced in ecstasy to a tribal rhythm on the mounds of fallen mango leaves. Initially, she would hum while sweeping, but Ammu noticed her gradually changing. Kaliamma was quiet now, her eyes heavy with a shadow of depression. Ammu wondered if Kochuraman had scolded her for sleeping with her at night. On the day of their wedding, Ammu had a gut feeling that Kunjikkali was not the right woman for this ignoramus Kannali Raman, which she later discussed with Valiyachan.

"He is an orphan, my dear; that's why I arranged his marriage. I hoped that with a loving woman to care for him, he would become more humane. But alas, it's impossible to straighten the bent tail of a dog. You must also know that I had a selfish motive—I wanted Ammutty to have a mother's companionship. At least that much has happened ..." Valiyachan said with a deep sigh.

Seven

BEFORE KUNJIKKALI MOVED into Manthoppu, Ammu thought her school-going experience was like the fragrance and taste of a native mango—sweet yet predictably monotonous. But with Kunjikkali's arrival, the school transformed into a place where she could savour a variety of delicious, crispy snacks like *upperi,** *arimurukku,*† and *vada,*‡ all wrapped in dried plantain leaves and tied with plantain fibre. Each day became an exciting new adventure. The journey to school meandered along the lake shore, a merry trip involving drinking from and playing in the fresh waters of the lake and climbing the stone-cut stairs. Even the ancient country mango trees would bloom and shower sweet mangoes during the mango season. Tholan Gopi and the unruly Mudiyan Chandu were skilled at felling bunches of mangoes with a single throw. Every mango tree had been planted by Ammutty's Valiyachan. "To plant a tree is to repay a debt to our ancestors, who left us these precious trees we enjoy today. And planting trees is our duty to the generations to come," he lovingly reminded her.

---

* Sweet banana chips coated with jaggery and ginger
† A spiral-shaped fried snack made from rice flour
‡ Fried snack made from lentils

Kaliamma put Peshkarangunnu's advice into practice. In the northern yard, she prepared the ground around a coconut tree for growing red spinach, green chillies, eggplant and ladies' finger. Pumpkin and white gourd grew alongside *kanthari* (bird's eye chillies) and curry leaf plants. All plants flourished thanks to the manure compost and cow dung mixed with cow urine. A fragrant arch laden with a variety of flowers such as *kudamulla, arimulla* (both jasmine varieties), *parijatham* (gardenia), *rajamalli* and *chembakam* (frangipani) bloomed next to the porch. The bungalow was transformed into a lush garden home. Kali ensured Ammu Vaava's active participation in all activities, teaching her about gardening, thatching palm leaves, and even milking cows from an early age. Thus, Kaliamma became not only Ammu's mother but also her teacher.

In the ensuing days, the constant calls for "Kalippennu", or Kali girl, echoed throughout Manthoppu Bungalow. Manthoppilamma summoned Kunjikkali to prepare a vessel of hot water and keep it ready in the bathroom, along with medicated oil and specially formulated shampoo. Manthoppilangunnu called her to prepare the ground by the lake for his gymnastics. Kochuraman would yell, "*Ediye!*"(eh woman), from the cowshed for her help in managing the volatile cows. And from the backyard would come the shrill voice of that vile Eenampechi Parothi, calling for Kunjikkali to help in hoisting a basket of dry leaves onto her head. Then it was Yashodamma's turn, from the kitchen, to call out "Kalippenney" for help with cutting vegetables. Even Vasukuttan required her assistance in mending the broken string of bells around Manikandan's neck. Kunjikkali responded to each call without hesitation or complaint.

Every night, she would tell Ammu Vaava stories until she drifted off to sleep. These weren't just myths and legends of the past, but also tales from the present. Vaava would often enquire, "Where did you learn these stories, Kaliamma?" That's how she came to hear about Kumaran Mash, known as Comrade Kumaran, who had hidden in Kali's hut at Ambumala for more than a year. Manthoppilangunnu arranged for his stay there and ensured all the supplies he needed were delivered by Thala Pulayan Ayyan. He was one of the best teachers in Kuttanadu. And the times were such that it was tough for those with a conscience to remain mute.

Though the villages remained prosperous with lush green expanses, vast paddy fields, and granaries filled with mounds of paddy straw soaring like hills, the peasants and workers starved due to exploitation by greedy landlords. Those in power showed callous disregard for the famished labourers. There was a severe scarcity of food during the Second World War. In the Cherthala region alone, nearly 21,000 workers perished from starvation.

Kumaran Mash spent his days indoors, immersed in books. He resembled a hermit with his unkempt beard, long hair, and magnetic eyes that seemed from another era. Tall and fit, he ate little but drank plenty of water. At night, he washed his clothes in the nearby brook. Kunjikkali found him to be a fascinating character. He would affectionately call her *koche*, or kid. When her parents went to work, she roasted tubers and prepared the earthen pot for gruel. After winnowing the rice, Mash would cook it in the earthen pot, tend to the cooking fire, and help with all her chores. He was a remarkable man, his eyes brimming with compassion.

In the nights, he would sit on a coconut stump by the brook. After the day's labour, workers from all twelve hamlets would bathe, dine, and gather to listen to Kumaran Mash. When he spoke, he transformed into a different person; you could no longer see the calmness in his eyes.

"The workers must unite to demand their rights. Do not hesitate to pick up arms if necessary. That's what happened during the Punnapra Vayalar uprising. How long can one live under someone's boots? The peasants and coir workers attacked police stations and government offices en masse. Their aim was not to kill but to endure and survive. They were determined not to pay boat tariffs and other taxes. With raised fists, they chanted slogans like *"American model Arabikkadalil* (American model in the Arabian Sea)". The army of the poor fought valiantly, resisting armed police with spears. Both sides suffered heavy casualties, but the toll was higher among the workers. Suspects were shot, and many were arrested; their fates unknown. Many fled for their lives, and I am one of them. That night in Kainakary, I emphasised the folly of fighting and dying without proper organisational support or weapons to oppose the royals supported by the British and the despotic dewan, Sir C.P. Ramaswamy Iyer. For now, retreat and regroup to resume the fight with augmented courage. Root out slavery from your hearts and lands so that you can live as humans with rights. Raise your voices. Let us heed the words of Ram Manohar Lohia, who said a stagnant

Kumaran Mash addressing the workers

society is an eternal curse. And remember the advice from the Bhagavad Gita: 'Silence is death'."

Kumaran Mash lacked the hubris of a scholar and had no desire for recognition, yet he spoke with conviction. His words ignited fire in the eyes of his listeners, and their fists trembled with rage.

Meanwhile, Kunjikkali sat on a wooden plank in the yard, listening to all of this. She also learnt the freedom song he had taught everyone:

Let's go; let's march forward, dear brothers,
Is that not the battleground we see?
Let us march to that battleground
and wage war for our land.
Let those with lathis beat us.
Let them empty their guns upon us.
Let's go; let's march, my dear brothers.

Kali would passionately sing the song, with Ammu joining her.

Eight

THOUGH AMMU VAAVA was now a teenager, her playfulness remained the same. She talked like a chatterbox and flitted about like a butterfly. She smiled like a blooming flower and sang merry songs. Ammutty was the budding flower and singing bird of Manthoppu. The only annoyance was Ammamma with her curses and outbursts. Complementing the mother was her youngest son, Madhavan, or Kunjammavan, as he was called. He was the *Kochangunnu*, or junior lord and master, of the bungalow. He studied in Thiruvananthapuram and visited home only during holidays. A chip off the old block, he was very much like his mother in his views and perception of everyone around him. He fancied himself the supreme commander of everyone, a trait missing in his father, Peshkarangunnu. Being a fiery orator, handsome and financially well enough to indulge his friends, thanks to his family's wealth, helped him rise as a student leader in college. In public, he would passionately advocate for equality, gender rights, freedom as one's birthright and other progressive theories.

However, at Manthoppu Bungalow, he reprimanded Parothi for addressing him as Kochangunnu. "Ammas and Pillas, such as Yashodamma and Kunjanpilla may call me

Kochangunnu. But Pulayas must address me as *Thambran*." Unlike his father, who believed in *Loka Samastha Sukhino Bhavanthu* (May all beings everywhere be happy and free), the son didn't have the heart to digest this principle. He often scolded Kunjikkali, suspecting that she was being given extra leeway in managing household affairs. He found fault with her smile, but when she did not smile, it was treated as an offence too. She was forbidden to be seen with a broom when he was around, believing it to be a bad omen. He even suggested that since Ammu was no longer a child, she should not require nighttime company, and Kali should sleep with her husband. He had just turned twenty, but he behaved as if he were the patriarch of the household.

Kunjammavan had a close bond with Kochuraman, who acted as his immediate proxy in power. Kaliamma soon discovered the secret of their alliance. Kochuraman frequented Vattavila Vasanthi's toddy shop in the evenings, and always returned with a bottle that he secretly stashed in the farmhouse for Kochangunnu. Though Manthoppilangunnu was aware of this, he ignored it as it was common among the Cheruman Pulayas, both young and old, to unwind with drink after work or during festivals like Onam and Sankranthi. The elders of the community also indulged in chewing tobacco or betel leaves secretly if restrictions were imposed, habits ingrained over generations like thorns deeply embedded. Plucking them out suddenly could only cause injury. Getting rid of these addictions required patience, time and persistent effort, with education essential for fostering change. Education is also about cleansing the body and the

Comrade Madhavan speaking in a public meeting

mind. Through his words and actions, Manthoppilangunnu reminded his fellow humans of Gandhiji's belief in education as a means of character building.

Kunjammavan eloquently preached about revolution, yet his actions were clouded by his aristocratic authority. Despite his impassioned discussions of global history, particularly the French Revolution's ideals of liberty, equality, and fraternity, he definitely did not wish for any social change. As "Comrade Madhavan", he quoted Marx and Engels, emerging as an aggressive leader among students. While his father disapproved of such lip service, his mother enthusiastically supported him. Manthoppilamma always held her favourite son in high regard, often demeaning her elder son, whom she considered an effeminate fool for leaving his family under the influence of an "alien woman"—a bitterness she harboured until her death.

Manthoppilamma failed to acknowledge a father's steadfast love for his beloved son. Instead, she supported all the wrongdoings of her younger son and justified his behaviour. However, Manthoppilamma was unaware of her pampered son's fraudulent actions, both in the city and the village. She was a mother so blinded by affection that she failed to see her son's dual nature. Ammu always felt relieved when Kunjammavan returned to Thiruvananthapuram after his vacations at Manthoppu. Kaliamma, on the other hand, was never bothered by his pretensions or silly commands. Her face remained as serene as the surface of a pristine lake. Only much later did Ammu realise that hidden within that tranquillity were unimaginable and unfathomable whirlpools.

Nine

IT WAS *AAVANI,* also known as *Chingam,* the first month of the Malayalam calendar. The air was imbued with the sweet scent of *thazhambu,* or screw pine flowers. This fragrance always transported Ammu back to when she was two years old, sharing the Onam feast with her parents. Ammamma would recount the three types of *payasam** they savoured on *Thiruvonam,* the main feast day. However, on each Thiruvonam, she would also begin her ritual of lamenting her daughter's tragic fate, cursing those responsible for her merciless death. As a result, Valiyachan, partaking in the festive meal with everyone, often grew melancholic listening to Ammamma's sorrowful outbursts. He would stop eating, wash his hands, and retire to the southern verandah to find peace of mind.

After the Onam exams in Class VII, Ammutty was free to explore the woods with Kunjikkali and spend leisurely moments conversing with the serene Mother Lake. She wrote verses inspired by the pristine lake and relaxed on its sandy shores. Meanwhile, Kochuraman had pretended to be ill and remained bedridden for the past week, leaving all chores,

---

* A pudding made with rice, milk/coconut milk, sugar/jaggery, and spices

from cleaning the cowshed to milking the cows, to Kunjikkali. Unable to resist the alluring fragrance of kaithapoo carried by the southern breeze, Ammu hurried past the kadankunnu towards the bathing ghat.

It was dawn, and the sun had yet to rise in the sky. A gentle breeze wafted in from the east, carrying the sweet scent of thazhambu. Ammu walked towards the eastern direction, drawn by the fragrance. Amidst a grove of kaitha trees, she spotted a cluster of thazhambu reaching out to embrace the early sun. As she crawled through the small screw pines and climbed the larger ones, thorns mercilessly pricked her from all sides. Despite the pain, she continued her quest.

Suddenly, a stern and commanding voice abruptly halted her progress: "*Penne* (you girl)! Why are you wandering through the kaitha forest so early in the morning? The area is full of snake nests, and you risk stumbling upon one. Come down immediately!" Ammu was startled. For a fleeting moment, she forgot the sharp pain coursing through her body. "*Who dares to speak to me with such insolence in this secluded shore within my domain?*" she wondered.

Glancing over, she spotted him just beyond the kaitha grove, reclining on the sandbar by the lake, his legs leisurely dipping into the water. "What did you just call me? Was I named on your lap to address me as such? I am Ammu Devu Pilla of Manthoppu."

"*Pilley*, it seems I'll have to bring you down and lay you on my lap. You are covered in bruises and bleeding," he replied, his tone laced with amusement as he stood up. He was as tall as a blooming male screw pine and stood as unbending as a bamboo. His demeanour reflected both courage and a hint of wry humour. Stepping closer, he said, "Come down, girl!"

However, Ammu found herself trapped, unable to ascend or descend, and fear began to grip her. The burning pain from her bruises had become almost unbearable. Towering above her, he didn't need to climb to reach her. With his strong right hand, he grasped her, while with his left, he plucked the kaithapoo. Gently, he lowered her onto the sandbar. Blood seeped from the numerous cuts below her knee-length skirt. He washed away the blood with water from the lake, assuring her of its potent disinfectant properties. Though it stung, the pain became more bearable with the tender touch of his fingers.

"I was trying to pluck the kaithapoo because it carries my mother's scent," Ammu explained, struggling to hold back her tears. He comforted her, using his towel to gently clean her legs. "It's alright. Now wash your face and return to the bungalow, princess of Manthoppu." As he launched his boat into the lake and stepped aboard, he added with a warm smile, "The next time you want a kaithapoo, don't venture into the grove ... I'll fetch it for you. You can find me here every day at this time."

As the boat drifted smoothly across the lake, he retrieved the snare net from the water and dropped both small and large catches into his vessel. She stood there in awe, feeling as if the intoxicating fragrance of kaithapoo had somehow mingled with his scent. Both of them wore the protective armour of green thorns, yet underneath, their delicate leaves concealed soft, shy yellow petals and pollen grains.

Ammu covered the thorns with leaves and hurried back to the bungalow.

At the kadankunnu, Kaliamma was busy cutting grass and herding cattle. Ammutty rushed to embrace her. "Look at this! Smell it. A boy plucked this for me, Kaliamma; he came to fish in the lake." Then, she recounted the entire story in a single breath. Kaliamma offered her some water and said, "Vaave, drink some water first. He seems like a good person, whoever he may be. He saved you from a fall."

That night, before she fell asleep, Ammu posed a question to Kaliamma, "Who is good? Who is bad? How can we tell the difference between them?"

"Good people are compassionate," Kaliamma replied thoughtfully. "They offer help in times of trouble and avoid unnecessary gossip. They are gentle with children and would never hurt them. Bad people, on the other hand, turn a blind eye to the suffering of others. They are selfish and might blame you for entering the grove if you were bitten by a snake. Moreover, bad people don't hesitate to harm children, especially girls. Vaava must never go near such people."

Ammutty tucked a petal of the kaithapoo under her pillow, now enveloped in the scent of the bold boy intertwined with the sweet fragrance of her mother. A strange sensation came over her. Kaliamma joined her for the night, and holding onto her, Ammutty whispered, "I will return tomorrow to pluck more flowers. Their fragrance is mesmerising..."

Aware that no more thazhambu were in bloom, she still wanted to meet him again. So, the next day at dawn, she ventured into the screw pine grove and spotted him reclining on the sandbar, gazing up at the sky. She called out "Hoi" to grab his attention.

"Which forest is Ammu Devu Pilla headed to today?" he teased. "Come over here. You can join me if you like. I'll tell you a story." She made her way down and settled beside him, her ears perked up in anticipation of the story.

"This is vaanarakkulam. A monkey dug this with its tail. Humans and monkeys are part of the same family. They are our ancestors. You're in Class VII, right? Have you studied the theory of evolution by Charles Darwin?"

"*He is well-read and impressive,*"Ammu thought.

"This lake and its shores don't belong to Manthoppu. The fish in these waters, all these trees, plants and flowers—they belong to everyone. Snakes have the right to nest and prey here. They don't care if you're the princess of Manthoppu; they will bite if provoked. Wouldn't it be wise to wait until the sun is up and shining before setting off on your adventures?"

Ammu looked at him curiously and asked, "In which class are you studying? What do you do? What is your name?"

"I have completed 6th grade, and I'm a fisherman. My name is Raju, and I'm from Thekkekara. If you have any further questions, we can save them for next time. The fish are already in my net, and I need to take them to the market." She watched him until his boat disappeared from her view. Over time, their meetings and conversations became regular occurrences. His stories were boundless and captivating, painting her days in a myriad of colours. They were unlike anything Ammu had ever heard before.

Ammu watching Raju's boat gliding across the lake

Ten

IN POOKKAITHAYOOR, ONAM was a celebration of flowers. Along all four shores, the woods burst into full bloom. Children engaged in friendly competitions to gather flowers for the *athapookalam* (intricate floral sketches) that adorned the entrances of their homes for ten days. They sought beyond the usual *tulsi, sivanaruli, ashokathetti, shanghupushpam, mantharam, jamanthi* or *hanuman kireedam,* which were common in their home gardens.

On the morning of *Attham,* the festival began with the humble offering of *thumbapoo* to adorn the head of the legendary King Maveli. It was not chosen for its extravagant colour or fragrance but for its simplicity. On the second day, it was the sacred Krishna Tulsi. As the days went by, the floral tapestry expanded with vibrant additions. Children delighted in embellishing the *pookalam* with petals of native flowers like *mukkutti,* multi-coloured wild *thechipoovu, kadali* (also known as *kalambatti*), *kinginipoovu,* and a host of other festive season blooms. They engaged in spirited competition, scouring the entire forest for flowers to create the most beautiful floral floor arrangements. For the elders, Onam marked the harvest season.

Children making *athapookalam* (floral carpet) during Onam celebrations

By *Pilleronam** in *Karkkidakam*,† the elephant yam and pumpkin would be ready for harvest. At Manthoppu, it was a season of abundance. Peshkarangunnu celebrated Onam by distributing all essentials to households across the four lands of Pookkaithayoor, from rice and cereals to plantains, vegetables and coconuts.

However, what disappointed Ammutty wasn't any of this. On the day of *Uthradam*, the first day of Onam, when the common folk who toiled in the paddy fields and farmland visited Manthoppu with gifts of bananas and native vegetables, they were given new clothes, rice and money. It was Ammutty's responsibility to distribute *onakkodi* (new clothes) to the children. Yet she never received any new clothes herself, and she couldn't fathom why Valiyachan acted this way. Unable to contain her curiosity any longer, she finally asked Valiyachan why she did not receive any new clothes for Onam.

"For school-going children, Onam is their school reopening day. On that day, we celebrate with new clothes, an umbrella and such items," Valiyachan explained. With the inauguration of the Achyutha Vilasam School and all the children of Pookkaithayoor starting their education there, Peshkarangunnu shifted the annual onakkodi ceremony for the children to the school reopening day. He did this as an incentive to encourage all children to attend school.

However, the arrival of Kunjammavan for the Onam vacation dampened the festive atmosphere at the bungalow. It

---

* A mini Onam celebrated for children, 28 days before *Thiruvonam*
† Last month of the Malayalam calendar

felt as if the place had come under martial law. Yet, Kunjikkali remained the same. She was assigned the additional task of organising *Kochambran's* bookshelf. It was only later that Ammutty understood the reason behind accompanying Kunjikkali to the room while she tidied up and arranged his books. During that Onam, Kaliamma disclosed to her that Kochambran had a tendency to misbehave and was considered a pervert.

Among Ammutty's "child brigade" marching to school, there was just one girl, Lalita, the daughter of Viswambharan who owned a provision store at Bhagothimukku. Ammutty affectionately called her Lalithechi, being older than her. Lalita possessed a loving nature and an attractive physique. One day, as she arrived late for class, Lalita was playfully serenaded by the Malayalam teacher Gopala Krishnan singing, "*Vannu Lalithe, Neeyen Munnil...*" (Lalita, you have finally come before me). Ammu found it amusing to observe Lalita's reactions, but she was puzzled by Lalithechi's blushes, bashfully doodling on the floor with her toe, or smiles at the sight of Kunjammavan.

During that Onam vacation, Lalithechi paid Ammu a visit. She sat next to Kali on the steps and exchanged pleasantries as Kali combed Ammu's hair. From his room on the western side, Kunjammavan passed by them twice on his way to the kitchen, where he asked Yashodamma for water. Yashodamma reminded him of the *karingali** water kept on his table. "But I need *jeeraka* water. I'll come back after you have boiled it," Kunjammavan replied. When he returned a

---

* A medicinal herb

while later, Ammu noticed him winking at Lalithechi, who responded by acting coquettish. Ammu was clueless about what was transpiring between the two of them.

"Some men are like this, like male dogs sniffing around bitches," Ammu overheard Yashodamma say to Kaliamma in the kitchen. But Kaliamma paid no attention to such gossip. She never flirted or acted coy with anyone; her interactions were always straightforward. That night, Kaliamma hinted at the reason why Kunjammavan hovered around the kitchen like a hawk.

"Some men feel a weird thirst upon seeing women, an unquenchable desire. Kochuraman has that thirst too. Vaava will come to understand this in time."

Ammu wondered why the kaithapoo was neither used in floral carpets nor offered in ritual oblations. Kaliamma always had a story to explain everything, and this one involved the trinity of Brahma, Vishnu and Maheshwara (Shiva).

"Once, a dispute arose between Lord Brahma and Lord Vishnu about who was the greatest among them. They went to Lord Shiva for a resolution. He pointed at an enormous vertical pillar and asked them to find its end in both directions. Thus, they embarked on their quest. After aeons of searching, a disheartened Lord Vishnu admitted defeat to Lord Shiva. However, Lord Brahma decided to lie and claim that he had found the end of the celestial pillar.

"To support his false claim, he sought the help of a kaithapoo that he found en route. He asked the kaithapoo to testify to Lord Shiva that he had succeeded. In return, he promised to elevate it as the divine flower of the heavens, to which the flower agreed. Thus, both Lord Brahma and the kaithapoo falsely testified before Lord Shiva. However, Lord Shiva was aware of the deceit and cursed Lord Brahma never to be worshipped as one of the trinity for lying about finding the boundaries of an infinite universe. The kaithapoo, complicit in the falsehood, was also cursed never to be used in oblations."

Manthoppu celebrated Onam in a grand and festive manner. People would gather to partake in the Onam festivities. There were tug-of-war competitions at the kadankunnu, where Vasukuttan would effortlessly pull Kochuraman to his side with the rope. Schoolchildren enjoyed *kilithattukali** on the vast playground of the Achyutha Vilasam School. On the porch of the bungalow, women would merrily immerse themselves in traditional art forms like *thiruvathirakali, pennuchodyam,* dancing joyously to songs such as '*Ashakoshale Pennundo, Cherukoshaalum Pennundo,*" and *mudiyattam*. Daivathal would faint after a bout of *mudiyattam*. When Parothi began singing the *Thiruvathira* song "*Pankajakshan Kadalvarnnan Vasudevan, Jagannadhan,*" in her shrill cricket-like voice, Kunjikkali would intervene by hushing her and taking over. Then, the sweet and melodious voice of Kunjikkali would fill the air as she sang the song and kept the rhythm with a mallet in her hand.

Kunjammavan, being a late sleeper and riser, didn't hamper Ammutty's morning routine, allowing her the freedom to step out and do as she pleased. In a matter of days,

---

* A traditional game of Kerala played between two teams of five people. The referee is called a kili.

Raju had become her playmate. His openness, confidence, knowledge and caring nature drew Ammu closer to him in an inexplicable manner. Despite their recent acquaintance, they both felt as though they had known each other for ages, their stories flowing endlessly.

One day, Ammu shared Kaliamma's tale of the cursed kaithapoo with Raju, seeking his guidance on how to lift the curse and restore her mother's scent. As the secretary of Pookkaithayoor's *Jalamatha Grandhashala* (library), Raju was busy with the library's Onam celebrations. Yet he never took a single day off from his family's fishing trade. On the dawn of *Uthradam*, he docked his boat on the sandbar where he usually met Ammu. He had a mysterious smile as he approached her with his hands hiding something at the back. "Show me your right hand," Raju said, placing something on her palm. She sniffed—it was thazhambu wrapped in a teak leaf. "This is my Onam gift for Kunjava ... the thazhambu that blooms in Thekkekara in the month of Chingam."

Kaliamma called her Vaava, but Raju made it even sweeter by calling her Kunjava. She was thrilled!

"The cursed kaithapoo is not ours. The kaithapoo of Pookkaithayoor will never lie," Raju said, placing a petal in her braided hair.

"Kunjave, I now place this petal here as my offering. And thus, it is redeemed!"

Eleven

AMMUTTY GREW UP enchanted by the scent of the kaithapoo, which now carried a human touch. During their holiday encounters, she learned more about Raju. This was before the Achyutha Vilasam School had been established. Raju had to walk 12 km to attend school, yet he managed to pass his Class X examination with a first class. In those days, it was rare for someone to even clear the Class X exams. However, he lacked the means to continue further education. During that era, the prevalent aspiration was to complete Class X and then build physical strength akin to a wrestler's (*Sixthum Gusthiyum*). Raju, however, chose a different path, picking up his oar and embarking on a career as a fisherman. He proved himself adept at his craft, ensnaring every fish that crossed his path. He had no rush to catch all the fish in a single day; he simply aimed to earn an honest living without resorting to begging.

Raju possessed a voracious appetite for books, prompting him to establish the Jalamatha Grandhashala for people like himself who lacked the means to purchase books. He recognised that the writings of great men and women were perennial sources of wisdom like the mother lake, carrying precious lifeblood for the brain. Raju mobilised the village's youth and collected as many books as possible. Every evening, he opened the library, transforming reading into a celebration and organising special programmes on certain occasions.

Raju's father, Kattiprayi, had earned a living by selling fish in the local market. However, he underwent a transformation when he joined the Salvation Army, converted to Christianity and adopted the name Abraham. He became an evangelist, preaching sermons at village junctions, hoping his son would follow in his footsteps and join the Salvation Army. Kattiprayi even aspired to send Raju to the Salvation Army school in Thiruvananthapuram for higher studies and then to college in the capital city. However, Raju declined his father's wishes, firmly believing that he could attain salvation through his chosen vocation. This was the philosophy of the teenager, who was an avid reader.

"Why should one abandon their work just because of conversion to another religion," he argued. The village libraries served as a blessing for impoverished students who lacked other resources for tutoring or supplementary learning. Raju demonstrated to Ammu that books could open doors to larger worlds. Gradually, she, too, began to embrace the fascinating and illuminating concepts that Raju shared with her.

It was the dawn of the Renaissance in Travancore, marked by significant events such as the Temple Entry Proclamation, Vaikkom Satyagraha, visits by Mahatma Gandhi and the teachings of revered figures like Sree Narayana Guru and Chattampi Swamikal and a host of progressive thinkers and activists. While the Savarna upper castes played a pivotal role in initiating social change in northern India, it was the Avarnas, the backward castes and the Dalits who catalysed the awakening of Travancore to the need for social reformation. Ayyankali was a pioneer among them. Ammu listened to Raju in great awe; his narratives felt like a natural extension of the stories of Kumaran Mash, as recounted to her by Kunjikkali.

He spoke with ecstasy about the world's first democratically elected communist ministry under Comrade E.M. Sankaran Namboodiripad, which came to power in 1957. Simultaneously, he brimmed with rage as he denounced the class traitors masquerading as progressive movements, who subverted democratic governance with their so-called "liberation struggle". Those days were filled with both joy and substance. With each passing day, Ammu's initial impression of Raju remained steadfast—truly unique. They never ran out of topics to discuss. Sometimes, as they rowed on his country boat and drops of lake water splashed on her, Ammu would spontaneously recite a few verses: "To swim like a fish, to fly like a bird". Raju would gently brush her flowing hair aside and whisper in her ear that Kunjava would one day become a famous poet.

The next day, he would bring Changampuzha's poems and with a smile on his lips, alter the lines from "Ramanan" to "And yet, my Kunjave, this world we see is not the world we fancy". The call *Maattuvin Chattangale* (change the system) by poet Kumaran Asan always stirred his passion. He would confidently declare, "If the system does not change, we must change it!" His explanations of the history of the

Raju and Ammu rowing a country boat

global revolutions, beginning with the French Revolution, were challenging for Ammu to fully grasp.

Though his lectures began with Rousseau, who laid the groundwork for the French Revolution that sowed the seeds of "Liberty, Equality and Fraternity", and then moved to Karl Marx, the author of the Bible of the working class, *Das Kapital*, and the Russian Revolution, they usually culminated with Che Guevara. Guevarism consistently ignited a euphoric spirit within Raju. "Che Guevara was young and a physician, and his reforms as Cuba's minister of industries are immeasurable. But that warrior was never content, so he dedicated his life to the liberation of Latin America. His guerrilla war campaigns in the Bolivian forests were not just acts of resistance against imperialism; they were confrontations. These were the final words of Che Guevara as he stood amidst a hail of bullets: 'You can kill a revolutionary, but you cannot kill the revolution,'" he said.

"And isn't this similar to the cry of '*Inqilab Zindabad*' made by Bhagat Singh as he faced the gallows by the British?" Ammu interjected, recalling what Valiyachan had told her.

Raju would nod in agreement, yet whenever he spoke about Che Guevara, he transformed into a mythical serpent with a thousand tongues, much like Anantha. His eyes would gleam with inner fire. In Pookkaithayoor, he was known as Che Raju.

Twelve

SOMETHING STRANGE AND unsettling occurred in Ammu's life when she was in Class VIII. For two consecutive nights, she experienced excruciating pain in her abdomen. She rolled around in her bed, attempting to find relief by sleeping on her stomach. Ammamma attributed it to eating raw tamarind from the southern yard. Kaliamma made her drink ginger juice mixed with sugar. Even during school hours, she felt as if sharp knives were stabbing her stomach, and she silently endured the agony. However, Lalithechi, who sat beside her, noticed Ammu's muffled moans.

The lunchtime bell rang at noon, and the children scattered in various directions to enjoy their meals. As Ammu slowly made her way to the toilet, Lalithechi noticed three bloodstains on the white flowers of Ammu's yellow skirt from behind. She asked Ammu to go to the toilet and find out what happened.

Ammu removed her skirt, and upon seeing the blood, she began to cry, terrified and confused. Lalithechi comforted her, explaining, "Silly, this happens to every girl as she transitions from childhood to adulthood. It is called puberty. You are becoming a woman. It happened to me four years ago. Give me your skirt and wait here in your underclothes."

Taking charge, Lalithechi used a pinch of salt from her lunch pack to scrub away the stains, washed the skirt, fashioned a makeshift loincloth from her handkerchief, placed the remaining cloth inside, and secured it to Ammu's girdle. Although Ammu felt pain, embarrassment and distress, the experienced Lalithechi did what needed to be done, paying no heed to Ammu's emotional turmoil.

"Now wear this skirt. Since you're in pain, I will ask our class teacher, Susheela, if I can take you home."

As they walked along the lakeside, Ammu hesitated to jump over the touch-me-nots, fearing everything inside her body would bleed out if she did. When she reached home and saw Ammamma, Ammu felt as though she had committed a crime. However, she noticed a rare tenderness on Ammamma's face. "Don't worry, Ammu. You can go to the *theendamuri* (the isolation room) in the western corner. For the next seven days, that is where you must stay. Don't touch or get close to anyone," Ammamma instructed.

Ammu couldn't comprehend what crime she had committed to be sentenced to isolation! Kaliamma, who was cutting grass in the courtyard, overheard the news and rushed to the bungalow. "What happened to my Vaava?" she exclaimed. That was when Ammu burst into tears. Kaliamma gently caressed her head and held her close to comfort her. "My Vaava is growing up, and you will become a great woman one day. You always wanted to wear your Amma's clothes, right? My sweetheart is perfectly fine. There's nothing to worry about," Kaliamma assured with a loving and happy expression. She enquired if Vaava was experiencing unbearable pain and then led her to the room at the west end.

After ordering Yashodamma to prepare *payasam* and *neyyappam**, Ammamma retired to her swinging cot for a nap. Ammu, however, was confused and couldn't quite understand the logic behind celebrating the day on which her abdomen began to bleed as though it were her birthday. What hurt her even more than the physical pain, though, were the incessant restrictions and don'ts that were imposed on her:

- Do not run.
- Do not bathe in the lake.
- Do not go near the prayer room.
- Do not draw water from the well.
- Do not go to school.

Ammutty felt as though her childhood was ripped out, and she was deeply offended. To add insult to injury, Kunjammavan came with his own set of pretentious directives: "You should no longer be friends with boys. Stop fooling around, talking, or laughing loudly. You should behave like a modest woman now."

Valiyachan remained the same in his ways. At five in the evening, sitting as usual under the mango tree, he called Ammutty for their daily newspaper reading session. He ignored Ammamma's stern gestures, warning him against asking Ammu to come out and sit close to him. When he enquired what was wrong with the child and whether she had

---

* Sweet rice-based fritters fried in ghee

Ammu being comforted by Kaliamma in the isolation room

any ailment that hampered her reading ability, Ammamma furiously stormed off without a reply.

As she lay on the grass mat over the coarse rope-woven cot in the theendamuri, both mentally and physically exhausted, Ammu asked Kunjikkali, who was sitting on a small wooden seat on the floor, "Kaliamma, how and when do boys become men?" Startled for a moment, Kunjikkali then responded with a smile, "Boys become men when moustaches start sprouting on their faces."Ammu thought about Raju and his moustache, which extended downwards on either side. She remembered him having a hint of a moustache when they first met. "*So, he was already a man! That was why he could carry me down from the screw pine grove with such ease,*"Ammu thought to herself.

That night, she drifted off to sleep, breathing in the scent of that masculine kaithapoo.

For Ammu, those seven days of isolation were a novel experience. They were days without the joy of swimming or bathing in the lake, and running uphill with her clothes drenched. Instead, she now bathed in the bathroom, pouring lukewarm water over her body with a mug. There was a loofah and *thaali* (shampoo infused with medicinal herbs). Kaliamma scrubbed her back and towel-dried her hair.

On the seventh day, as Ammu returned to her eastern room after the ritual bath, she felt the gazes of everyone inside and outside the bungalow fixed on her like never before. She cared little for this newfound attention. Her only relief was that she no longer had to spend the night before the first of the Malayalam month in the *Nakshatra* (starry) bungalow in the eastern corner of Manthoppu estate. It was a thatched room, where one could view the stars through holes in the roof, hence its name. Sleep was elusive due to fears of venomous spiders, centipedes or rats that might chew on one's feet during sleep.

The vile Parothi, sent to keep Ammu company, would be fast asleep until Kaliamma arrived to soothe her to sleep. This ritual was insisted upon by Ammamma to ensure Ammu was the first person seen in the bungalow at the start of the month, before any inauspicious creatures could enter. Ammamma would awaken Ammutty, bathe her in cold well water, dress her in clean clothes and seat her on the porch. Then, she would bring a pinch of holy ash from the prayer room and smear it on Ammu's forehead. She would also present Ammu with one *chakram*,* which was perhaps the only bright spot in an otherwise tedious process. Ammu saved these coins in her piggy bank for bangles and balloons from the fair during the festival at Bhagothikkavu.

Now freed from this ritual as a menstruating woman, Ammu rejoiced when Ammamma asked Yashodamma if her grandchild had turned five. The burden now fell on Yashodamma's grandchild, liberating Ammu from the absurd early morning rituals. At night, she dreamt of Raju with his peach-fuzzed face.

Spending a week without seeing him made Ammu acutely aware of how deeply he had become a part of her life. Although the kaitha blooms were long gone, it was time for their friendship to blossom with the arrival of spring.

---

* A copper coin used in the erstwhile Travancore State

After a week, she underwent the ritual bath to purify herself. Kaliamma cleaned the room and sanitised the grass mat and cot with cow dung mixed with water.

Everyone was busy with their own tasks, so once she regained her freedom, Ammu rushed to the kadankunnu. From there, she spotted Raju's country boat by the channel. He was sitting on the sandbar, gazing deeply into the tranquil lake. She approached him slowly, without making a sound, and covered his eyes from behind with her palm. It was a precious moment, cherished for a lifetime. He embraced her lovingly and passionately, expressing how long he had waited for her. "Where were you, my dear Kunjave?"

Embarrassed, she struggled to find the right words. And then he gently covered her lips. "No need to say anything. I know ... At first, I was worried because I had not seen you; I feared you might have fallen ill. As I lost sleep and appetite, I decided to wait for Kochuraman at the toddy shop, as I knew he would come there for his evening quota. I bought him a bottle of toddy and took him to the lakeshore. After a couple of swigs, he began to tell me about all that was happening at the bungalow. He mentioned the Kochambratti couldn't touch anyone and was in isolation for seven days. Vaave, why didn't you come and touch me? Do you know how much I longed to touch you and hold you close to me ...

"What is the point of these rituals? They are another form of untouchability. Even Gandhiji, who travels across the country to eradicate untouchability, seems to have missed out on addressing this type of untouchability and the humiliating treatment of womanhood. Why must we tolerate and observe such obsolete superstitious customs? Those who created these foolish customs can observe them if they wish, but what right do they have to impose them upon others? This celebration with *payasam* and neyyappam was merely a proclamation to announce to the world that a girl in the family has transitioned into womanhood," Raju exclaimed with simmering anger.

"Kunjave, were you alone in the room?" His concern softened when she told him that Kaliamma had kept her company. "Ayamma is much more sensible than Kannali Raman and more educated than Comrade Madhavan. It would be more comfortable for her to sleep with Ammu than to have to spend the night with that obese fool. She's lucky. One day, I too will be blessed with that fortune. Whatever else may change, you will always be a Kunjava for Raju…" His eyes gleamed with love as he spoke.

Thirteen

FOR THE PEOPLE of Pookkaithayoor, the second most important celebration after Onam was the Kasturi Kunnil Bhagothi festival, dedicated to the mother goddess of Kasturikkunnu. Legend has it that the temple's origin dates back to when people clearing turmeric fields stumbled upon an idol of the goddess stained with blood. They stopped their clearing efforts and installed the goddess there, establishing the tradition of her worship.

The *para ezhunnallathu,* a festive procession of the goddess, spanned all four lands. It commenced with early morning rituals, including stopovers at the Manthoppu Bungalow, meticulously cleaned and prepared for the occasion. Ammu watched Kunjikkali prepare the ground. The floor was coated with cow dung paste, and adorned with ceremonial patterns drawn in rice flour and turmeric powder, with a lamp of five wicks and long incense sticks burning on a plantain stem. This marked the beginning of Ganapati Orukku.

A specially kept sack of paddy was carried from the granary to the lawn. When the priest arrived with the representation of the goddess, known as *Jeevatha,* on his shoulder, Manthoppilamma lit the lamp and camphor, and then filled the bushel with three palmfuls of grain. Following suit, Ammu performed the same ritual. Once the bushel was filled, the procession team took the remainder. Meanwhile, the priest blessed the family and home by sprinkling blessed grains on the porch and in the rooms, praying for abundant harvests and bountiful granaries in the years to come.

Gifts were presented to the priest and his entourage accordingly. The pyrotechnician received chakrams based on the number of fireworks ignited. Separate payments were made to the *nadaswaram** player and the rest of the orchestra, along with the accompanying children's band. After all the rituals and blessings, a grand feast awaited everyone at Manthoppu. With content hearts and satisfied stomachs, the procession team bid farewell and continued its journey.

The Kasturi Kunnil Bhagothi festival was like another Onam for the people of Pookkaithayoor. A highlight of this celebration was the ornate floats, a spectacle received with great enthusiasm. Residents from all four lands vied to showcase their exquisitely decorated temple carts or floats, known as *kuthira* (horse) and *kaala* (ox), accompanied by traditional percussion band performances, including the renowned *chendamelam*. The goddess, as *Jeevatha*, graced these impressive exhibits with her presence.

However, it was the grand entrance of the heavily adorned Manthoppilamma that stole the show and put all the other spectacular displays to shame. She would approach the massive, vibrantly decorated kaala sponsored by Manthoppu Bungalow, reverently touch its foot, and then summon

---

* A double-reed wind instrument from South India

The ox float during the Kasturi Kunnil Bhagothi festival procession

Kunjupilla, Vasukuttan, Kochuraman and other youngsters to lift the float. Thus began the *kaalayeduppu*, the ceremony of lifting the ox float, with all its fervor.

Chirutha and Panjami would whisper about Valiyambratti's radiant *suryavattakkammal*, the sun-shaped diamond earrings adorning her earlobes. Her neck was adorned with a thick gold necklace, an amulet, and a gold sovereign chain. She wore a white stone stud on her nose, and gold bangles graced her arms. Her fingers sparkled with a *palakka mothiram*, an expensive ring symbolising aristocracy. She dressed in a specially designed and embroidered handloom blouse, dhoti and *neriyathu* (upper cloth), finely woven at Balaramapuram. The women from poorer backgrounds stood awestruck, momentarily forgetting her haughty and vain nature. Angunnu, though not fond of such extravagance, remained silent at his wife's whims and fancies.

Angunnu organised a Kathakali performance on the night of the festival and tasked Kunjupilla, Vasukuttan and Kochuraman with booking the performers in advance. When they met Govindan Asan, the secretary of the Attinkara Kathakali Samiti, he presented them with options: "*Rukmini Swayamvaram, Dhakshayagam,* or *Keechaka Vadham*—which do you prefer?"Asan also briefed them on the expenses associated with each show. Kochuraman expressed interest in *Keechaka Vadham* (the slaying of Keechaka). Asan informed them it would cost Rs 3,000. Kochuraman jokingly responded, "Asan, you don't need to kill Keechaka. Just scare him off. How much will it cost then?" This remark annoyed Asan, who retorted sharply, "Get out! I am not auctioning any games here. I've heard of Manthoppilangunnu owning cattle herds, but I didn't know he had a donkey for a herder!" Kunjupilla hastily apologised, and they settled on booking *Rukmini Swayamvaram*.

Fourteen

AMMUTTY ALWAYS FELT that Kochuraman was not the right companion for Kunjikkali. She had even shared her concerns with Valiyachan, who defended Kochuraman, by saying that since he was an orphan, he had hoped that an efficient and caring woman in his life would bring about a positive change. However, Kochuraman's behaviour kept getting worse. He spent more time with Vasanthi, indulging in midnight toddy drinking sessions and picking fights with Kunjikkali upon returning. Ammu realised he was physically abusing her when she saw the palm print on Kaliamma's cheek. Every evening, after dinner, Kali would come to Ammu's room. Even though Ammu would joyously glide around like a dragonfly, she would lose her mirth upon observing the distress on Kali's face. Kali diligently carried on with her chores, but Ammu could sense Kaliamma's hidden despair. The young girl, now in Class X, had begun to feel her beloved mother figure's emotions deeply.

Though Raju was a stranger to her family and the upper class, he loved and cared for Ammu more than anyone else. She was the apple of his eye, and he looked after her with great care and affection, ensuring her safety during their walks and explorations in the woods and screw pine groves. He kept a watchful eye on her on the way to school and back.

Ammu and Kaliamma

Konthi, the dog of washerman Cheerukkutti, was a regular visitor to the school ghat during lunchtime. Cheerukkutti, who lived in a dwelling by the lake near the eastern slope of the kadankunnu, later moved to a house below the school on a ten-cent plot registered in his name by Angunnu. Ammutty and Konthi were childhood friends, and she always shared half of her lunch with the dog.

One afternoon, Konthi did not show up at school as usual. Instead, it was found at its usual resting spot under the cashew tree, foaming at the mouth and exhausted. When Ammu approached and patted it, the dog unexpectedly bit her leg, its two fangs tearing through her skirt. Terrified and startled, Ammu threw her lunch at the dog and fled screaming. Lalithechi rushed towards Ammu and held her close, while the other children panicked and ran back to school. Raju arrived at the spot in a jiffy and immediately washed the bleeding wound with soap. He then tightened a towel above the bite mark to stop the blood flow. "I think the dog might have rabies. I'll be back soon with the rabies healer. Lalitha, please escort Ammu to the bungalow," Raju said as he rushed to get the healer.

At the bungalow, Kaliamma immediately charred the bite wound to prevent infection. She used a heated pepper leaf, a mixture of three herbs and *murivenna** given by Ammamma. Ammu screamed out in immense pain. Soon, the healer, Chatthu Vaidyan, arrived. He prepared herbal medicinal

---

* A medicated Ayurvedic oil with anti-inflammatory, pain-relieving and analgesic properties

mixes for her and prescribed a *kashayam*,* which was a sour liquid that she had to consume for 48 days. Additionally, there was a seven-day treatment called *dhara*.† This was before the invention of the anti-rabies vaccine, and the only remedy at the time was traditional medicine.

Later, Ammu learnt that Raju and his friends pelted stones at Konthi and drove it into an abandoned well near Shappumukku (toddy shop junction). In a different story, the foxes of kadankunnu were said to have also leapt to their deaths into the same well on hearing Konthi's mad hollering.

Everyone at the bungalow was sad and terrified. It was one of those rare instances when Manthoppilangunnu appeared deeply tense. Even Manthoppilamma could be heard praying for the child's safety. Kaliamma kept a nightly vigil to ensure Ammu was not feverish. Each morning, Raju arrived to examine the wound and monitor its healing progress. Tenderly, he would kiss the bite mark, murmuring, "May any remaining poison transfer to me." Yet, there was one person who remained unaffected by all this—Kochuraman.

Kaliamma's eyes welled with tears whenever Ammutty spoke of Raju's profound love. One day, Kaliamma expressed her desire to have an affectionate and caring son like him. "Why haven't you given birth to a child yet, Kaliamma? I want a little brother or a sister," Ammu asked affectionately, tracing her little fingers over Kaliamma's belly.

"For that, one must sleep with a potent man. Kunjikkali is unfortunate in that regard, my dear," Kaliamma's voice

---

* A medicinal decoction
† An Ayurvedic oil therapy for head

quivered as she spoke. Then she exploded, "Kochuraman is neither a man nor a woman ... even that ox Manikandan would be ashamed to call Kochuraman Kannali‡." Ammu couldn't sleep that night. Kaliamma was brimming with a rage that she didn't understand.

Ammu soon realised that even her grandfather was disappointed with Kochuraman's behaviour. Valiyachan would talk about his plans to build a bamboo shelter on the kadankunnu—a place where one could change after a bath or swim in the lake, and rest. He also visualised it as an ezhuthupura in the future, where Ammutty could read and write surrounded by the lake on three sides, with fresh air and natural light.

Cheerukkutti's old shack on the eastern slope remained in a dilapidated state. It could be rebuilt with sturdy mud walls and robust doors and windows made of anjili timber, capable of withstanding harsh weather. Kochuraman and Kunjikkali also needed a secure roof over their heads. When Ammu moved to Thiruvananthapuram for her higher studies the following year, Kunjikkali would no longer have to sleep in the bungalow. Angunnu hoped Kochuraman would become responsible when it was time for him to take care of his own family. These were the immediate plans Angunnu hoped to implement.

The ezhuthupura was built in no time. It was a charming bamboo house. "Lightning won't strike this place," said Kaliamma. Ammu was happy; she could now feel the breeze

---

‡ Cattle

from the southern shore where Raju lived. She was also excited to see Kunjikkali's new home, and as soon as the work was finished, she accompanied Kaliamma to see it. The house stood on a plain near the lake, with a sandy lakeshore providing enough room space for Ammu to play. Later, Kaliamma dug a small pond nearby, explaining "Drinking water can seep into the pond, but there's no place as pleasant to live as where my Vaava is."

However, the real "drama" began soon after Kaliamma and Kochuraman moved to their new home on the slope. While living at the bungalow, Kochuraman had limitations on how late he could return home because he feared both *Valiyangunnu* and *Valiyambratti* and the repercussions of his late-night shenanigans. But upon moving to their home, he sank deeper into his nasty behaviour. Every night, he returned home drunk and abusive, demanding, "You barren Kali, open the damn door!" He would yell and bang on the open door frame, then order Kunjikkali to serve him dinner, finding faults with the fish curry and throwing the entire pot through the door. When Kunjikkali tried to stop him from smashing all the pots and pans, he mercilessly thrashed her with the skatefish tail kept in the corner.

One midnight, unable to endure the physical abuse any longer, Kunjikkali fled to the bungalow, spending the night in Manikandan's shed. When Valiyangunnu discovered this, he stormed to the slope and kicked the still-drunk Kochuraman awake. When he stood up, Valiyangunnu repeatedly slapped him—first on his right cheek, then the left, and again on the right—until he collapsed to the ground. Valiyangunnu also forbade anyone from even giving him water.

From then on, everyone at the bungalow regarded Kochuraman as a loathsome creature. Even the women, including those who had been jealous of Kunjikkali, such as Yashodamma, Parothi, and Panjami, were pained by the sight of the bruises and burn marks on her chest. The men scolded Kochuraman for his cruelty. A week later, Kunjammavan, who had been occupied with party meetings, brought Kochuraman before Valiyangunnu.

"Only weak men raise their hands against women. And you try to hide your insecurities by harming Kunjikkali. If I hear of even a grain of sand falling on her because of you, I will grab your arms, break your legs, and throw you out of the bungalow," Valiyangunnu declared, putting an end to Kochuraman's physical assaults on Kunjikkali. Unfortunately, his mistreatment then took a new, sharper form—spewing venomous words under his breath.

Fifteen

CLEARING THE CLASS X examination with a first class was a matter of immense pride in the villages, a rare achievement at the time. The rural students had limited exposure to knowledge, and Ammu's education went beyond textbooks. Kaliamma often reminded her of the valuable lessons she had learned from Kumaran Mash's classes, while Raju shared insights gleaned from his extensive reading. Valiyachan played a significant role too, regaling her with stories of Indian and Travancore history, and imparting wisdom acquired from his life experiences and learning, along with inculcating the habit of reading newspapers. It was no surprise that Ammu topped the local education district, even surpassing Raju, who rejoiced in her success more than anyone else.

It was Valiyachan's cherished dream to send Ammu for higher education. He considered his granddaughter the light and joy of his home. While he didn't insist, he held her close and said, "You should be smart like Devayani."

"Kunjava has outshone me, but this failure of mine has its grace. I want you to soar even higher than the sky," Raju said as he celebrated her victory by lifting her up like a child. Ammu felt conflicted about leaving him to pursue higher education. And even though he didn't want to say goodbye, he consoled both Ammu and himself, looking forward to their reunion.

Kunjammavan insisted on educating his niece at the Women's College, Thiruvananthapuram. The comrade, who set off revolutionary sparks in his speeches, quite ironically believed co-education was not befitting for those from aristocratic families. He showered her with heaps of advice, "Stay within the city; limit visits outside. If necessary, you can visit the temple once a week. Don't wander with friends, and don't waste time on poetry or stories." He even disapproved of her poems being published in magazines, emphasising, "You are here to study." However, Ammu wasn't keen on the notion of simply memorising everything taught by the teachers from the syllabus and then regurgitating it for an examination. Kunjammavan did another amusing thing: he introduced her to the hostel warden, who happened to be a distant relative, and ensured that Ammu received special attention at all times. But Ammu chuckled at his reluctance to let her share a four-person hostel room.

Ammu felt awestruck and intimidated on her first day at the Women's College, Thiruvananthapuram. Ammu Devu Pilla of Manthoppu Bungalow's high self-esteem melted away upon seeing the fashionably dressed city girls, some of whom arrived in fancy, new model cars. A car was a spectacle in her hometown—a rare sight. Ammu recalled how Sushila teacher once used a stick to disperse her young students just to see and, possibly, touch the car of the district collector, who had come to inaugurate the school's anniversary celebrations.

The Women's College, Thiruvananthapuram

Her first class was an English literature lecture. The professor, dressed elegantly in a white saree with red border and a matching red blouse, approached the pulpit with an air of confidence. Some students greeted her with a "good morning", but a dumbstruck and tongue-tied Ammu couldn't even utter that. Her gaze remained fixed on the teacher throughout the class. As the class began with a short poem, English words flowed gracefully, filling the room with a sweet melody. Despite topping her taluka in English, it seemed Ammu's language skills momentarily deserted her as she struggled to grasp the lesson. The teacher singled Ammu out, remarking, "The young lady in green, the beauty at the far left of the third row, please stand up. Have you not had your morning tea? Why are you drinking that ink?" The class erupted into laughter, and Ammu began perspiring.

Students from English-medium backgrounds appeared effortlessly fluent in the language, and she felt an overwhelming sense of inferiority. "*I don't belong here. Should I return to the bungalow?*" She spent the entire night grappling with these thoughts and reflecting on her mother, Devayani. Her mother had chosen simplicity over the allure of gold and the glamour of city life, consistently ranking first in every exam, winning first prize for her short story in the college magazine, and even publishing a poem titled *Ente Gramam* (My Village). Then there was Valiyachan, who had earned a name and respect for himself as an able and honest officer of the Hajur Kacheri. Ammu considered Raju, who took pride in his Kunjava being boundless like the sky. Finally, there was Kaliamma, who reminded her that after Valiyangunnu,

Ammu Vaava was the only one in the bungalow who dared to question why her community was so marginalised and degraded.

"I must study and reach a position of power. I must not extinguish all their hopes," Ammu resolved.

Rosamma from Pala was her roommate. Her parents lived in the United States, and she had studied in an English-medium school; hence, she was fluent in the language. "Could we please speak to each other in English from now?" Ammu requested. It was a matter of pride and accomplishment for Rosamma. This aristocratic beauty was asking for her help! Paying no attention to the other girls mocking them, they began their journey to become fluent in English.

Gradually, Ammu immersed herself in English literature, delving into collections far more extensive than her previous Malayalam readings, as vast as the deepest oceans. A desire to pursue higher studies in English literature began to take root within Ammu as she explored the world of short stories, poetry, novels and drama. She began to dream of pursuing a master's degree and eventually doing research in English literature.

Over time, her admiration for her teacher, the vibrant young lady who teased her on the first day of college, blossomed into a deep and enduring friendship. Sharada teacher even accompanied her to Manthoppu Bungalow, where she stayed for a few days. She enjoyed swimming in the lake. Later, she became Ammu's guide and guardian angel.

When the first term ended, Kunjammavan arrived a day late to take Ammu back home for the holidays. He made the excuse of having attended a political meeting in Neyyattinkara. Soon, his deceit was exposed—he had a secret lover in Neyyattinkara and he would visit her whenever he was in Thiruvananthapuram. He hadn't disclosed this to his mother, who trusted him blindly and shared a rather inseparable bond with him. They reached Manthoppu Bungalow too late in the evening, and Ammu was disappointed not to be able to meet Raju that day.

Valiyachan's face beamed with happiness, and Kaliamma's drained eyes glowed as she embraced Ammu. Sometime during the night, Ammu was stirred awake by dampness. She wondered, "*Is it raining? Is the roof leaking?*" However, she soon realised it was Kaliamma who was sobbing. Tears drizzled from her eyes like rain. "What happened, Kaliamma? Why are you weeping?" Ammu asked her anxiously.

"I feel like I'm falling, my dear. I want to leave this place, but I cannot and will not leave you. When you are away, I sometimes yearn to run away, but I don't want to be ungrateful to Valiyangunnu, so I stay ... Kali can't bring shame to the family. I count the days until Vaava returns, suffering in silence until then. I am torn," Kunjikkali explained her dilemma. Ammu understood that living with Kochuraman had become unbearable for Kunjikkali.

"I'll get a job as soon as I finish my studies. And I will live with Raju and Kaliamma. I'll beg and plead with Valiyachan for his permission. I don't care what anyone else thinks," Ammu assured Kaliamma.

She eagerly awaited the break of dawn and hurried to the lakeside. However, she didn't need to descend the kadankunnu because Raju was already waiting for her at the top of the hill. Both of them were anxious to avoid encountering Kunjammavan, so they slowly walked down the hill with their hands intertwined. The overgrown screw pine groves cast a soothing shade over them. Some of the screw pines had bloomed into fruition, while others sprouted anew, longing to bloom. Ammu, too, felt like a bud, ready to blossom. "When I couldn't meet you, I realised that the hope of seeing you again was what made life worth living," Raju said.

"I wasn't counting days, but seconds. The moments we've spent together, I treasured in my heart," responded Ammu poetically.

"My Kunjava has grown a bit tall," he said tenderly. Both of them felt that ten days were far too short to recount all the stories of the three whole months they had spent apart.

Raju had several plans and programmes to share with Ammu related to the Onam celebrations. For the next *Avittam*, the third day of Onam, Jalamatha Grandhashala was staging a play.

"It was Gopalakrishna Pilla Sir who selected the play 'Veluthambi Dalawa'. He was just waiting for an opportunity to play the role of Veluthambi Dalawa, the great patriot. He is even willing to bear all the expenses, so we have agreed. At least, we won't need to beg for donations. He has also donated some books to the library. But he won't pass for a gentleman. Once, that pervert misbehaved with a girl who had come to rehearse the welcome song, frightening her and causing her to run away. We consoled her and promised to stand guard in order to bring her back. And so, we have decided to give him the right 'treatment' for his nerve disorders," Raju said, explaining his plans to teach Gopalakrishna Pilla a lesson. He would never tolerate any misconduct towards women.

Ammu asked what he meant by the "right treatment", to which Raju replied, "I'll tell you once it's done. I'll be free after *Avittam*. Let us now row to all four shores and celebrate your arrival," Raju said excitedly.

Onam celebrations at the bungalow took place as usual. Ammu noticed Kunjikkali's subdued demeanour, lacking her usual enthusiasm. Even as Parothi sang in her cricket-like voice, Kunjikkali didn't intervene with her mellifluous voice or correct the rhythm when Panchami stumbled.

"What's happened to you, Kaliamma? Why aren't you paying attention to the songs or the dance? You didn't even seem to notice the break in rhythm," Ammu enquired.

"Hasn't the world itself lost its rhythm, Vaave? Mother Earth will restore balance after enduring as much as she can. We, too, must endure, just as Mother Earth does," Kaliamma replied stoically.

"Didn't you give your special 'medicine' to Gopalakrishnan Sir?" was the first thing Ammu asked Raju on *Chathayam* day.

"Of course, we gave him something he won't soon forget," Raju replied with a mischievous chuckle. And when he narrated the story to her, she couldn't resist bursting into laughter.

It was Raju who had rented the long coat to be worn by Veluthambi Dalawa. The night before the play, Raju had sewn a nest of red ants wrapped in a cloth inside that coat using just two simple stitches. The play started at 8 p.m. with the welcome song, followed by the famous *Kundara Proclamation*.

"Patriots ..." Gopalakrishnan Sir began, but before he could utter the next word, he scratched his back once. The next line was, "Now, it's time for open war!" and the disturbed red ants inside the coat began their attack. Soon, the itch spread all over his body, and he could barely stand still. The curtain was drawn before he could finish his speech, and he hastily discarded the coat. It took a while for the itching to subside.

"You don't need to hurry. We have plenty of time," Raju reassured Gopalakrishnan Sir.

To keep the audience engaged, the girl who had sung the welcome song proceeded to sing a patriotic melody while the pervert Gopalakrishnan Sir was taking care of his "itchy" situation. He refused to wear the long coat again, and resumed his role as Veluthambi Dalawa, wearing a *jubba* (a loose white kurta made of thin cotton).

"I had read about this trick some time ago and decided to use it to teach a bad teacher a lesson when the opportunity arose," Raju said.

When Lalithechi came with *payasam* for *Chathayam*, Ammu shared the story of Gopalakrishnan Sir and the "medicinal" red ants, leading them both to erupt in hearty laughter.

Like Ammu, Raju, too, adored Kaliamma. Whenever they met, he would share with Kaliamma how much he missed not having Ammu around. Their bond was similar to the comforting relationship between a mortar and *maddalam* (a traditional percussion instrument).

"She is such a wonderful mother. She calls me 'son' with such affection. My own mother never calls me so warmly. Those Dalit folks who have sacrificed their self-respect and honour should learn from Kaliamma. I had planned to give that moron Kochuraman a proper thrashing as an Onam gift in front of the toddy shop, but Valiyangunnu got to him first. The wound festers because it was left unattended when it was still fresh. Those who lack the will to stand together are scattered. My community, which degrades itself, should learn from ants that march together towards their goal," Raju eloquently shared with Ammu.

Then, the two of them parted ways once again, each preoccupied with their dreams of uniting and ensuring their separation was transient.

It didn't take long for Ammu to become a star at the Women's College, Thiruvananthapuram. Sharada teacher became her greatest supporter as she excelled in her studies of arts and literature. During breaks, Sharada teacher would invite Ammu to her room and introduce her to various books, opening up the world of English literature to her. Ammu didn't need to think twice about choosing English as her elective for her degree. For her, who was baptised in the eternal waters of the pristine lake, seeking knowledge came naturally.

Sixteen

AMMU DISCOVERED THAT Valiyachan had been admitted to the district hospital due to chest pain only upon her arrival in Manthoppu for Christmas vacation. Kunjammavan, who had come to pick her up, remained silent about it. Ammu sensed something amiss when she reached the bungalow. Valiyachan, who usually enjoyed his evening siesta beneath the mango tree, was conspicuously absent from his armchair. Whenever Ammu returned home, her first stop was always beneath the mango tree to meet Valiyachan before entering the house. Ammu washed her feet and face, changed her clothes, and then proceeded to the southern room. There, she found Valiyachan, who never napped during the day, lying in bed with his head resting on a folded pillow and his eyes shut. As Ammu approached, he opened his eyes and smiled affectionately upon hearing her call, "Valiyachan, I am here."

Thulamazha, the northeast monsoon, was pouring down in all its fury on that ominous night when Valiyachan suffered from severe chest pain. Just two days earlier, he had received devastating news via telegram: "Sivasuthan Pilla has tragically passed away in an accident. He fell under a moving train while trying to board at Victoria Station. Arrangements have been made to keep the body in the mortuary for two days.

Please inform us if you plan to attend the funeral." This telegram had been sent from Bombay by Babu, a close friend of Sivan.

On receiving this shocking news, Peshkarangunnu, known for his resilience, lost his usual calm demeanour and sank into his armchair. Kunjupilla rushed to fan him, while Yashodamma brought a glass of warm jeeraka water to soothe his distress.

In stark contrast, Manthoppilamma received the tragic news of her firstborn son's death with apparent detachment. Her response was marked only by a deep sigh and a simple remark: "What can we do now? It's not easy to travel such a long distance. Besides, Angunnu, in his advanced age, cannot undertake such a journey." With these words, Rudrani Thankachi retired to the *arappura*.

Deeply troubled, Angunnu knocked on the door of the *arappura*. When Rudrani Thankachi slowly opened the door, he encountered a dispassionate woman.

"Rudrani, may I take tomorrow morning's train to Bombay to see Sivan's face one last time? His wife and our two little grandchildren need our support. Rudrani, my heart isn't as strong as yours to abandon them while I am still alive," Angunnu pleaded. However, Rudrani remained unmoved by his appeals.

"If you consider your daughter-in-law and her children more important than me, Angunnu can go. But make sure you book a return ticket to join my funeral!" she declared firmly, before shutting the door of the arappura in his face.

Padmanabha Pilla (Valiyangunnu) grieving over his elder son's death at the lakeshore

Valiyangunnu sank into deep despair. Over those two days, the weight of his son's loss bore heavily on him, extinguishing his thirst and appetite alike. On the day of his son's funeral, Valiyangunnu went to the lakeshore early in the morning and sat there, meditating on a rock. The Mother Lake absorbed his streams of tears into her bosom, and those streams then gave way to a heartfelt cry echoing across the entire lake. The western winds carried the anguished father's grief over the vast Arabian Sea to the funeral grounds in Chembur, Bombay.

The next day, Raju couldn't hold back his tears as he recounted to Ammu the sight he had witnessed from behind the screw pine grove—Valiyangunnu crying his heart out. "I couldn't bear that sight, Kunjave! I walked up to him and offered my support to that great man, helping him stand. Then, silently, I walked beside him all the way to kadankunnu, sharing his pain and sorrow over the loss of your Valiyammavan (maternal uncle). He rested his right hand on my shoulder as he settled into the wicker chair on the verandah of the ezhuthupura, and I sat on the parapet.

"Since he had been missing from the bungalow for quite some time, Kunjupilla came looking for him. As Valiyangunnu rose to leave, he patted my shoulder and gently said, 'You can feel the pain of a stranger, young man. I appreciate your empathy. What is your name?' When I introduced myself as Raju, he looked at me with great affection and said, 'Raju, my son, one day you will become Raja, the King'. With those words, he walked away. I can still hear him. I carry his words in my heart. Be brave, Kunjave.

Manthoppilangunnu is a great man, and this land needs him. He won't leave us all so easily."

Valiyangunnu didn't leave soon, but he was bedridden after experiencing severe chest pain that night. Meanwhile, Kunjammavan was on his southern tour. Pattupadi Vishwambharan came with a car and took Angunnu to the district hospital, where tests revealed blockages in his arteries. Since Angunnu was averse to surgery, he was given medication instead. Those five days at the hospital further weakened his spirits. Always living an independent life, he struggled to adjust to the many restrictions. He could no longer engage in anything that might strain his body, thereby disrupting his daily routine. His pre-breakfast walk to the lake, yoga, swimming, and other morning activities came to an abrupt halt. Angunnu was fond of long bicycle rides, but those were now forbidden too. With his beloved activities taken away, he began to contemplate the meaning of mere existence. It wasn't just his heart but his mind that felt imprisoned. Even his routine of reading the newspaper every evening became a dull affair. He started spending most of his time in bed, eyes closed, disinterested in his surroundings. Occasionally, his spirits lifted briefly in Ammutty's presence, but soon the shadow of despondency returned.

Seventeen

AMMU WAS RELUCTANT to leave Valiyachan when her Christmas vacation came to an end. She believed Kunjammavan's request to extend her stay by two weeks, approved by the principal and hostel warden, stemmed from his love for Valiyachan. But that wasn't the case. The mother and son were busy conspiring about their next move.

Valiyachan had to legally transfer extensive land holdings, including the kadankunnu and nearby areas, the Aayirappara Kandam in Thottinkara, and the ten-acre property of the Manthoppu Bungalow, into Ammamma's name. This was to ensure that the vast wealth would remain under her ownership in case something happened to him, potentially safeguarding it from the widow and children of their eldest son, Sivasuthan.

Kunjammavan, having seen the world and its complexities, warned Ammamma about the looming dangers, which increased her anxiety. As her insistence grew stronger, Angunnu yielded to her wishes, saying, "May your desires be fulfilled, Rudrani. Give me two days, then summon vendor Nanu Nair and prepare the documents as you wish. Pay the fees and bring the registrar home; I'll sign the papers."

The following morning, Valiyachan spoke to Ammu. "My dear, let's go to the lake. It's been a while since I took a dip in the waters of Mother Lake. Let's visit her. A slow walk won't harm my heart; it would only aid my blood circulation." As they descended the kadankunnu, he gently held Ammutty's hand. "My girl has grown strong enough to support Valiyachan's arm. The joy of immersing oneself in these waters is truly profound." Each time he took a dip, Ammu felt reassured that if anything went wrong, she had Raju waiting behind the screw pine grove, ready to dive in and rescue Valiyachan within no time.

After his bath, Valiyachan settled into his chair in the ezhuthupura. Kunjupilla had already cut open tender coconuts from the bunch on the coconut tree in front of the writing hut. Valiyachan and his granddaughter savoured the sweet, nectar-like tender coconut water together. He had something on his mind that he wanted to share with Ammutty.

"Ammutty, you once asked me why I tolerate the whims and arrogance of your Ammamma. I have told you part of the story before. She is the daughter of Achyuthan Pilla Sir, who entrusted her care to me. She was his treasured child, and I am bound by his trust to always look after her for his peace of mind. I have known Rudrani since she was a little girl. Hubris and stubbornness were her innate qualities. Her mother, Karthiyayini Thankachi, and all the women of her family, from Koyikkal Kovilakam, valued their land and wealth above all else. The expansive farmlands and fields stretching beyond the horizon, along with the serfs dependent on them, made them feel all powerful.

"In the era of *marumakkathayam* (matriarchy), the great-uncle of the family held supreme authority, while the father's role was merely nominal. If the uncles were under the sway of powerful matriarchs, then the nephews had to find subsistence within the family serving them. When Rudrani's grandmother's elder brother married an avaricious woman from Ottasekharamangalam, Karthiyayini Thankachi didn't get her rightful share of the family property. This led to a series of never-ending legal battles. Her father, Velayudhan Pilla, made the courts his second home. But they lost the case, and her father never returned home. He died there on the verandah of the courthouse.

"Karthiyayini, who went home for her delivery, did not return with her child. She was furious that her husband Achyuthan Sir did not lift a finger to help her despite his connections with the royal palace as a tutor. Achyuthan Sir treasured knowledge over material wealth and didn't prioritise property matters. Hence, his mother-in-law held him in disdain, deeming him useless. For Karthiyayini, her mother's word was final. Initially, she was reluctant to return to her husband with their newborn because she believed it would be meaningless to live with a man she considered worthless. However, when the *ameen** came to enforce the court order and post the notices at their home, Achyuthan Sir personally went to bring his wife and child back home. Meanwhile, Karthiyayini's mother refused to live with her

---

* A confidential agent, especially a minor official of the judicial and revenue department

son-in-law and chose the path of devotion, joining an ashram (a monastery) in Parassala.

"Achyuthan Sir never harboured ill feelings towards his wife; he was deeply attached to his daughter as well. Yet, not a day passed without Karthiyayini lamenting her lost glory. Her face and actions reflected her bitter disappointment and indignation. She breastfed all these 'qualities' to her daughter. Karthiyayini struggled to manage domestic life without servants attending to her every need. Her tongue could only deliver swear words. Even when she fell severely ill with pneumonia, she adamantly refused hospitalisation and eventually succumbed, coughing blood. Rudrani lost her mother before she turned ten.

"Achyuthan Sir raised his motherless child with excessive affection. When he wanted me to marry her, I was well aware of her pigheadedness and greed for material wealth. Yet, nothing changed my love for her. She was the first girl I ever spent time with. Initially, she intimidated me, but over time, we grew close. I have loved her since her childhood to this very day. At first, I believed she was beyond my reach, and it was essential to ensure that she was always kept high on a pedestal. Only then would I have honoured my commitment to my guru, my mentor.

"I have lost two of my children. Could it be an ancestral curse? It is a curse to lose one's children while you survive. It must be the cost of the many sins that our forefathers committed generations ago—the sin of denying land to those who tilled it; the sin of failing to shelter those who built for us; the sin of starving those who sowed, grew, reaped, and filled our granaries with grain. I have done many things to atone for these sins, despite all the opposition I've had to endure.

"Sivan and Devayani, too, wanted to follow in my footsteps, but that generational curse touched them as well. Madhavan has his mother's blood, so he continues to indulge in sin. My heart aches when I think about future generations and the suffering they will endure because of his misdeeds. You are my only hope, Ammutty. Kaliamma is your source of strength. Education isn't just about securing a job; it's meant to make you a better human. You should write and become the voice of change. Tomorrow, I am drafting the deed. May Rudrani be at peace. May her wishes be fulfilled," he concluded.

The following day, Nanu Nair arrived to draft the deed. Valiyangunnu, though tired, insisted that half of the assets would go to Ammu, as Devayani was the rightful heir.

"How is that possible? Everything should be divided equally into three parts—for Amma, for me, and my sister's share should go to Ammu, noting that she is a minor," argued Kunjammavan.

"One-third of the assets should be registered in Ammu's name. As she is a minor, her uncle Madhavan should be appointed as her guardian. Her share can be released to her upon her marriage, for which her uncle will be responsible," Ammamma intervened, with Nanu Nair seconding her. As a result, six acres and 70 cents of land in kadankunnu, where the ezhuthupura was located, were registered in the name of Ammu Devu Pilla, with Uncle Madhavan taking on the role of her guardian. A provision was added to transfer ownership of the property to Ammu upon her marriage. Valiyachan signed the deed half-heartedly, his thumb trembling as he impressed it onto the document. The Manthoppu Bungalow and its surrounding property in Ammamma's name were registered as a gift deed to Kunjammavan. With the formalisation of his last will, Ammu couldn't help but notice a look of "everything is finished" on Valiyachan's face. And she was right.

It was a Friday night, and the lake lay still, perhaps sleeping cosily under the chilly blanket of *Makaram* (the winter month). Kunjupilla, Angunnu's faithful steward, came to Ammu's door, panting and urgently awakening her. "Angunnu is taking his last breaths. He has been calling for Ammu." Startled, Ammu quickly followed Kaliamma. Kunjikkali quickly fetched water from the *kindi* (a spouted water pot) in the pooja room, carried it in a folded jackfruit leaf, and handed it to Ammu. But before the water droplets could reach his half-opened lips, the soul of Manthoppilangunnu departed from his body.

The sun rose late the following morning, and the foggy lake remained still. It was the day when the entire village of Pookkaithayoor wept. Villagers gathered en masse to catch a final glimpse of their beloved and esteemed Peshkarangunnu. Daivathal, Panchami, Nangeli and Thevi cried aloud, performing the traditional *opparu* (lamentation of the Dalits singing the glorious deeds of the departed). Tears streamed down the face of Ammamma, who had remained strong until the *vaykkari* (the ritual of dropping rice into the mouth of the deceased).

Kaliamma held Ammu tightly as she was brought forward to pay her respects to her beloved Valiyachan. She

Ammu performing the last rites of her grandfather

kissed his closed eyes one last time and whispered in his ears, "Valiyacha ... tell Ammutty what to do now before you leave forever." The scene was heart-wrenching for all who witnessed it, except Kunjammavan, who appeared unmoved, though a hidden sense of relief was evident. As Kaliamma guided Ammu to the eastern room, Ammu saw Raju standing by the trunk of the *soorankudymaavu* (a multi-branched mango tree). Feeling his eyes on her, Ammu found solace in knowing that she was not alone in her grief. She struggled to hold back her tears as she made her way to her bed.

At night, Ammu was startled awake by the sound of footsteps she thought belonged to Valiyachan. Kaliamma consoled her, saying that Angunnu was with her in spirit, which was why she could hear his footsteps. She continued to encourage Ammu to aspire to become a great human being like her Valiyachan—a compassionate soul.

The day after the *sanjayanam* (a ritual observed five days after a person's death), Ammamma summoned both Kittan Jolsyan, the astrologer, and the priest. She sought their detailed guidance on all the *bali* (sacrifice) rituals that Kunjammavan needed to perform. Since Angunnu passed away on a Friday, the astrologers predicted the possibility of more deaths in the family and provided a comprehensive chart of rituals to rectify this fate. However, Ammu was well aware that Kunjammavan was unlikely to bother with any of these rituals.

Ammu felt abandoned, sensing that the bungalow had lost its soul. Concentrating on her studies became increasingly challenging. She wandered aimlessly through the woods, crushing the touch-me-not plants that lined her path. As she walked, a sharp *kattara** pierced through her rubber sole and into her foot. *"Let it hurt for a while,"* Ammu thought, oddly finding solace in the pain as she continued limping forward. However, the thorn continued to burrow deeper. She leaped up and grabbed the rings hanging from the *kanjiram*† tree, where Valiyachan had once performed his daily gymnastics.

Observing her desperate actions, Raju quickly rowed his boat to the shore and, upon landing, asked her, "What are you doing there, Kunjave? This is no time for adventures. Don't you realise you might fall if you try to cling to those rings? You could break your knees. Don't you want to return to your college?"

"Come, sit here," he urged, gently positioning her close to him. "What's this? Your foot is bleeding! Oh no! It's the kattara thorn; it's poisonous." Raju first tried to pull the thorn out using his fingers. When that didn't work, he used his teeth to pull it. After cleaning the wound, he plucked Siam weed from the nearby thicket and squeezed its juice onto the cut. "Go back to the bungalow. Kaliamma might know what to do to prevent infection," he said. As she walked home, leaning on his shoulder with one leg on the ground and the wounded one held aloft, she silently marvelled, *"He is my greatest blessing."*

---

* A long, hard, poisonous thorn
† Nux vomica tree; often referred to as poison nut tree

"I'll accompany you as far as the kadankunnu ... Should I carry you?" Raju asked.

"That's not necessary; I can walk. What if someone sees us?" she replied.

"What's wrong with that? 'Kunjava stepped on a thorn and couldn't walk, so I carried her. Why should that concern anyone?' I will explain clearly to anyone who asks." With that, he gently lifted her up and placed her on his shoulder, as if plucking a flower.

"This isn't how you show your love for Valiyachan. Hurting yourself would only cause him pain. He initiated changes at the Manthoppu Bungalow as well as showered blessings upon the people of Pookkaithayoor. The most significant one is the Achyutha Vilasam School. What's even more remarkable than establishing the school was his decision to hand it over to the government, making it public property. Kunjave, let's continue what Manthoppilangunnu started. Look, I've brought a book today, *The Story of My Experiments With Truth* by Mahatma Gandhi—the life Angunnu aspired to follow."

Raju fetched the book from his boat and handed it to her. Ammu fondly remembered Valiyachan taking her to meet Prime Minister Jawaharlal Nehru when she was just a schoolgirl. People had gathered along the sides of the national highway to catch a glimpse of him. Young girls welcomed the PM in front of the Chavara Rare Earth Company with *thaalappoli*, a ceremonial procession where women carried *thalam*, or plates, filled with rice, flowers, and lit lamps to welcome esteemed individuals. Everyone was dressed in white khadar skirts and dresses. The most beautiful girl among them had greeted Chacha Nehru with a rose garland.

Meanwhile, Ammu, clad in a long blue dress, felt self-conscious and hid behind Valiyachan, feeling embarrassed. Valiyachan reassured her that attire didn't matter and lifted her high over his head, pointing out Nehruji to her. At that moment, the open jeep carrying Nehru slowed down briefly. Chachaji, standing in it with a smile and joined palms, removed the rose garland from around his neck and tossed it towards Ammu, and he didn't miss. It landed on Ammu's neck! Before the jeep moved on, Valiyachan ran towards Chachaji, who bent down, patted Ammu's cheek, and asked her something, which Valiyachan later recalled as "How are you?" It was an encounter that Valiyachan cherished with immense happiness and pride.

Upon returning to the bungalow, Kaliamma hung the garland on the picture of Ammutty's mother. The next morning, before heading to school, Ammu proudly wore the garland again, eager to show it to Raju. However, when she returned from school that evening, the rose garland was nowhere to be found because Yashodamma had cut out the lemon from it to prepare lemonade for Kochangunnu. "Ammamma made me do it …," Yashodamma said, explaining her helplessness. Kaliamma rushed in on hearing Ammu's scream. That night, Ammu refused to eat dinner. Valiyachan called her close to him and gave her *Letters from a Father to His Daughter*, a book written by Nehru when he was in jail. He told her, "Do not cry, my dear. Read this now."

Ammu began reading it that night and thought, "*If only my parents had written me such letters!*"

During her first year of college, which didn't require exams, Ammu spent most of her time in the ezhuthupura, reading extensively and writing a few pages. It was during this period of intense sorrow that Ammu slowly evolved into a writer.

Eighteen

MANTHOPPU HAD LOST its soul with Valiyangunnu's passing. The estate had fallen eerily silent, resembling a graveyard. Even the once lively and chattering women had lost their vivacity. Kunjupilla, Vasukuttan, and Pachu had all lost their moxie. Manthoppilamma herself had shed her grandeur and power with Angunnu's departure, becoming a subdued figure. Her once earth-shattering footsteps, perpetually held high head, and commanding voice had all mellowed.

Rudrani Thankachi, who had previously controlled even the slightest leaf's movement, now showed disinterest in everything, leaning on Madhavan to make decisions. Ammu wondered if her Ammamma's previous pomp and show had merely been an outward projection of everything that Valiyachan chose not to indulge in! However, the frequent visits of Kittan, the astrologer, who now came every week instead of once a month, revealed her grandmother's fear of death.

Since Angunnu passed away on a Friday, the astrological remedy to prevent further untimely deaths in the family involved Kochangunnu performing ritual sacrifices for the departed soul on a certain day every month at the temple in

Thiruvallam, Thiruvananthapuram. Kunjammavan would travel to Thiruvananthapuram for this ritual and then proceed south to Neyyattinkara, where he would stay for the next two days.

Yearly treatments for Manthoppilamma's rheumatism proved ineffective. Even Vadakkunnathala Aasatti's traditional medicines offered no relief. To compound her woes, a herbal concoction she tried ended up upsetting her stomach. Now, she struggled with both an upset intestinal system and rheumatism. One fateful night, a severe headache left her paralysed and bedridden. Kunjammavan brought a gastroenterologist from Thiruvananthapuram to examine Ammamma. Further investigations revealed that she was afflicted by advanced pancreatic cancer. The doctor recommended managing her pain with painkillers and keeping her at home.

Though Ammamma had never appreciated Kunjikkali before, Kunjikkali diligently attended to her, ensuring she received timely meals and medicines while maintaining a clean environment to prevent bedsores. Meanwhile, Kunjammavan became even more absorbed in his public activities. Kaliamma confided in Ammu that during her final days, Ammamma had been distressed by her son's lack of concern. "My son can't spare any time for me. He shows more concern for others than his own mother," she lamented.

Sadly, Ammamma never knew that her dear son, Madhavan, was incapable of expressing an emotion called love. It was only a year after Manthoppilamma's death that the world discovered Madhavan Pilla of Manthoppu was a hypocrite who didn't hesitate to deceive his mother to get things his way. Ammamma's passing occurred when Ammu returned home for the summer vacation after her second-year exams, barely a year after Angunnu's death. The women whispered about Kittan's prophecies, while the people of Pookkaithayoor worried about who would be next!

With Ammamma's passing, Kunjammavan assumed control. He spent more than half of each month in Thiruvananthapuram. Meanwhile, Kochuraman's distinctive bracket-like posture and gait gained momentum. He spent most of his time eating and drinking at Vasanthy's toddy shop and became an assistant at the bootlegging enterprise owned by Vasanthy's partner, Sahadevan. Kochuraman was responsible for burying and later digging up the *kodakalam* (spirit pot) from the paddy field behind the toddy shop. However, only Sahadevan knew the exact proportions of *koda* (spirit/liquor). As Vasanthy stoked the furnace, Kochuraman filled the distilling pot with water and briskly bottled the alcohol that dripped through the pipe from the distilling pot. Vasanthy's shack bustled with children, as she had four of her own, and Kochuraman took care of the younger ones.

During moments of intoxication, Kochuraman would taunt Kunjikkali during his occasional visits, saying, "You barren Kali, I now live in a place filled with children. How wonderful it is to watch them laugh and play! I live there now, so I don't have to look at your disgusting face anymore." Kunjikkali would go into hiding in a nearby thicket while Kochuraman, after sobering up, would fall asleep on the verandah of the hut and then head to the bungalow at daybreak. Kochangunnu had sold all the milking cows, but the ox, Manikandan, remained unsold because he couldn't fetch the expected price. His cart lay rusting in a corner.

The bungalow and its assets lay neglected, prompting Kunjupilla, Pachu, and Vasukuttan to seek other jobs. Only Yashodamma remained in the kitchen. Kochuraman earned a living through bootlegging and maintained the farmhouse for Kochangunnu. Kali made ends meet by gathering and selling coconut spadix and dried coconut leaf rolls at the teashop. She collected the dry leaves in a shed, burned them, and sold the ash manure to local farmers. Fiercely independent and self-reliant, she never begged for anything from anyone. Duty was paramount for her, and she meticulously cleaned the bungalow and its surroundings, ensuring not even a speck of dust gathered on the floor of the ezhuthupura.

"This was once the residence of a great man, the bungalow of Manthoppilangunnu. When my Vaava completes her studies and secures a job, all this will change," Kali reassured herself.

Kunjammavan would visit Manthoppu only to sell coconuts from the property and take whatever he could to Thiruvananthapuram. He made his presence known by hosting lavish parties and get-togethers with abundant alcohol at the farmhouse. During those nights, Kali stayed awake, armed only with her iron blade for protection.

One night, Sahadevan joined Kochuraman on one of his drunken midnight visits. Kali tightened her grip on the blade as she cautiously opened the door. When Kochuraman tried to force his way into the room, she raised her blade at him.

"If you dare to take a step inside this hut, I'll cut both of you to pieces," she screamed in a fury reminiscent of goddess Bhadrakaali. Sahadevan, sensing danger, ran for his life.

"I am your man, and I have authority under this roof. You're my wife, and I'll do whatever I please," Kochuraman asserted. Kali, though seething with anger, refrained from resorting to extreme violence. Instead, she grabbed the stingray's tail and flogged him left and right, returning each beating she had endured with interest.

"I won't behead you and throw you in the lake because I don't want to pollute my Mother Lake, you stinking Kannali. Never dare to set foot here again! If you cross me again, I will chop off your lame leg," she declared firmly as she kicked him out of her verandah and into the yard.

"Now go and look after someone else's bastards, and drink yourself to death. Take this with you as well," Kali roared, yanking out the black thread that symbolised their wedding vows and throwing it at his face. With that, their marriage came to an end, and so did Kochuraman's trips to the hut.

"Kochangunnu, she's has lost her mind. She used a stingray tail to beat me mercilessly and threatened to hack me to death. I can't handle that crazy barren woman anymore," Kochuraman complained to Kochangunnu, showing his bruised back and chest.

Kochangunnu questioned Kunjikkali about her actions, and she responded with a direct demand.

"Can you stop Kochuraman from going to the toddy shop and bootlegging? Can you prevent him from bringing bottled

Kunjikkali hurling the *thali* at Kochuraman

alcohol to this farmhouse? If you can do that, then I will live as his obedient wife. When Valiyangunnu was alive, we had someone to take care of us, and I tolerated everything out of respect for him. But you have shown us no care. A *thambran* (lord) is someone who feeds us and ensures our well-being. You are not a thambran," Kali lashed out.

Nineteen

THE RESULTS OF the BA exam were announced, and newspapers carried the story of Ammu Devu Pilla of Manthoppu Bungalow securing the first rank. Ammu, however, was far from elated. She felt a pang of sadness because her beloved Valiyachan, who would've been the happiest person to hear this news, was no longer around to partake in her triumph. She did feel relieved to have earned a scholarship to continue her studies because she knew that Kunjammavan was utterly unreliable.

Kaliamma, who had been sweeping the yard, quickly washed her hands and approached Ammu. Taking Ammu's hands in hers reverently, she said as though offering a prayer, "Valiyangunnu must be watching this from above. He must be elated now."

Ammu hurried to the lakeside where the tranquil Mother Lake welcomed her with a serene smile, its surface spotlessly clean and beautiful. Ammu took a mouthful of the sacred water, feeling a moment of peace. Raju arrived earlier than usual, clearly excited about the outstanding success of his beloved.

Pointing to the kaitha, still waiting to bloom, Ammu told Raju, "Look at it. This kaitha should bloom before I leave so I can take it with me in my bag."

"If it doesn't bloom before you leave, then I'll bring it to you when it does," Raju promised her.

Raju's friend Paakkaran had got a job as a *khalasi* (porter) in the railways, so he would travel to Thiruvananthapuram every Saturday to meet Paakkaran. However, Raju's main reason for the trip was always to see Ammu. He would stay at the railway quarters in Poojappura. In the evenings, Ammu and her friends would explore the city, often visiting its numerous temples, as Ananthapuri is renowned for them. They would walk from their hostel at Vazhuthacaud to the Ganapati temple and then head straight to the Indian Coffee House near the University College. A masala dosa there cost two rupees, and the joy of sharing it among their group of four was a memory they cherished dearly.

Raju eagerly awaited their arrival there. Ammu's friends often playfully teased Raju, insisting that he treat them to *masala dosa*. They were close friends who could clearly see the intense relationship between Ammu and Raju. After leaving the lovebirds at the coffee house, they would proceed to the church in Palayam, and from there, they would visit the Hanuman temple. It was a time when young people didn't need to belong to a particular religion to pray together.

Ammu and Raju would gaze into each other's eyes, reflecting the yearning they had felt during their time apart, followed by the sheer joy of their reunion. As they settled into a quiet corner of the coffee house, they would begin their never-ending conversations. But before the stories could reach a climax, Ammu's friends would return with sandalwood, saffron paste or holy oil smeared on their foreheads. Raju would greet them with a parcel of four masala dosas. It was no wonder that Ammu's roommates eagerly awaited Raju's visits.

Initially strangers, Ammu's roommates had hesitated to engage with one another and maintained a certain formality. However, after a week of sharing a room, they found themselves unable to stay silent. Even those who had initially insisted on a curtain partition to change their clothes eventually stripped them off without inhibitions. Rosamma was the one who shocked everyone.

The bathrooms were situated at the southern end of the long verandah. Just beyond the compound wall stood a men's lodge, where mischievous men were always ready to leap over. While watching the girls of the women's hostel go to college, they would shout out various female names: "Leele, Radhe, Kausalye, Philominey, Suhraa ..." The list of names seemed endless, and if a girl happened to glance in their direction, it served as confirmation that they had correctly identified her name!

The lodge also housed cocky lads who dared to leap over the hostel walls to peek at young women bathing. Once, Rosamma heard someone whistling while she was showering. When she looked up, she saw a pair of eyes scanning her every move through the air vents. Terrified, Rosamma screamed and ran naked through the corridor from the south end to the north, dripping with water! She hurriedly grabbed a shawl from a random room and wrapped it around her shoulders as she rushed back to her own room. This incident earned her the nickname "Kuli-scene Rose" (bath-scene Rose). Raju and Ammu always had a good laugh while recollecting that story.

It was on one such day that Ammu and Raju's free-flowing love was disturbed and threatened. Kunjammavan, who had been celebrating the entire previous night with his friends, gorging on fried chicken legs and guzzling alcohol, woke up late and looked out from the kadankunnu. His gaze fell upon the "blood-curdling" sight of his niece chatting and flirting with Kattiprayi's son, the Dalit boy, from the south shore. "Ammu, come here at once," he bellowed. But Ammu didn't appear bothered or scared by his thundering command. Kunjammavan climbed down the hill.

"What the heck is this? The daughter of Manthoppu is chatting with such tramps and beggars," he shouted.

Raju's face darkened with anger. "Comrade Madhavan, who are these tramps and beggars? I ask you because I haven't heard of such terms in the communist terminology," Raju said with indignation.

"Who's your comrade? Be careful when you meddle with gentlemen, you penniless convert. Don't you dare seduce our girl," a furious Kunjammavan threatened.

"Comrade, I shall leave now. I addressed you so because I read your name as Comrade Madhavan in the notices announcing public meetings. I also want to make it clear that no one here is trying to seduce the girl of Manthoppu. I have known her since she was 12, and I know she does not belong to your category of the tempted lot. I forgive your idiocy because you are her uncle. Don't assume I am leaving because I don't have a befitting reply for you. And if you don't know me, then take note and remember this name: I am Raju; Che Raju."

It was both a loud declaration and a warning.

With resolute steps, Raju boarded his raft and rowed away.

"You are no Che. You are a cheat," Kunjammavan yelled, panting as he climbed the hill. Ammu stood there for a while, head bowed in embarrassment and humiliation.

Kunjammavan's rage continued unabated even after he reached Manthoppu Bungalow. He launched into a lengthy monologue about Manthoppu's superior pedigree, expressing his fear of the disgrace that would befall the family due to Ammu mingling with lower castes. He concluded with a stern warning to her:

"You are not to see him anymore. I had warned my father several times about not extending leeway to girls. But he left us after raising you to be so independent and educating you with the hope that you would become a collector one day. You claim to be writing poems on the lakeshore, but you go there to flirt with him. And he dares to row to our shore to romance you. He is even capable of swimming across the lake. Such is his wicked boldness. But I'll drown him in the same lake," Kunjammavan declared aloud, ensuring Kunjikkali heard him.

"*It's fine for you to woo low-caste women working in the fields and to sleep with those cherumis (young Dalit girls) that Kochuraman brings to the farmhouse at night. I am a BA graduate, and I know all the spicy tales my hostel friends used to share*," Ammu thought, wanting to voice all of this and more, but she held her tongue.

Kunjammavan also threatened Kunjikkali. "Ammu is a grown-up girl. She should not be left alone in the woods or the kaitha groves. Ammamma took care of all that. I can't stand guard at the bungalow. I have important work to do in Thiruvananthapuram," he asserted. Kunjikkali simply crooned. "You crooning folk, you are good for nothing!" Kunjammavan said mockingly before preparing to depart for his affairs in Thiruvananthapuram.

Raju and Ammu continued to prove that nothing could stand in the way of true love. And the opposition from a hypocritical uncle was met with sheer determination.

Ammu decided it was best to pursue her postgraduate studies at her alma mater, surrounded by teachers and friends she knew. With results still pending, she found herself with ample time for long sleeps cradled by Kaliamma and moments spent with Raju. Ammu was not in a hurry at all.

She had a break until the month of Chingam, when the kaitha would bloom again. Since there were no workers around, Kaliamma's sweeping and cleaning chores stretched until noon. By then, Raju would be back after selling fish on his bicycle. During one of her solitary explorations through the woods, Ammu stumbled upon the *kadanguha,* or fox cave, stomping across the touch-me-not shrubs and being beaten by the hot sun. It was a home for the foxes, sheltering them from rain and sun alike. They would howl from there at dawn and receive responses from foxes on the other shores. This is how the hill got its name—kadankunnu.

Ammu recalled Valiyachan's nostalgic tales about the disappearance of the kadan howls from the hills. Valiyachan was equally concerned about foxes, dogs, cattle, birds and humans alike. *"Yet, why did he suffer?"* Ammu started brooding. *"Why was my mother, Devayani, burned to death? Why did Valiyammavan fall and die under the train?"* she wondered. In his last days, Valiyachan had lamented a decline in ancestral virtues as the cause of all these maladies. *"But why should generations bear the burden of their ancestors' misdeeds?"* Countless unanswered questions troubled Ammu deeply.

"Kunjave, are you doing penance inside the cave? Come out," Raju's call nudged her awake. Tears welled up in her eyes upon seeing him. "Everyone has left, leaving Ammu alone." "I am with you, my Kunjave," he reassured her, holding her like a child and comforting her with gentle pats on her shoulder. "Come, wash your face," he said, leading her to the lakeside. Scooping up water, he cleansed her tear-streaked eyes and dried her face with the towel draped over his shoulder. It was during this unplanned, extended vacation that Ammu truly saw Raju's heart. He gently soothed the endless agony of his orphaned Kunjava with care and affection. With his lips, he absorbed the dampness in her eyes.

Ammu began teaching Kaliamma the alphabet at the ezhuthupura. Valiyachan had tasked her with educating Kaliamma, but the illiterate Kaliamma was already a book of wisdom. Every utterance from Kaliamma resonated like the wisdom of Mother Earth, evident in the way she stopped Kochuraman from felling the kaitha grove.

"The kaitha fence around our Mother Lake prevents soil erosion. This earth, the sky, the water, the songbirds, the animals, the insects, the butterflies, the bees seeking nectar from the flowers, and the plants—all are children of our abundant Mother Earth," Kaliamma declared. "The pristine lake is the offspring of Mother Earth. The slithering snakes, the kadans of the kadankunnu, the rustling tweeters playing with dried leaves, the small fish in the lake, the kingfishers that prey on the fish, the *kalluran* (red-eyed crow pheasant), along with the green grass and wild trees—all are nourished by the lake's 'mother's milk'. One doesn't need to give birth to have children; fostering them is enough," she continued.

"They all find sustenance by drinking this water, the elixir of the lake. We humans must befriend them all. We should neither harm nor fear anyone. Instead, we must coexist. We must live and work, purifying our minds and our bodies," Kaliamma concluded.

Ammu paid heed to Kaliamma's doctrines while Raju signalled his presence by lighting a torch into the skies from across the shore. Kaliamma, in turn, continued her stories.

"I raised my baby brother when I was very young, carrying him on my hip and feeding him rice gruel. Before the birds woke up chirping, our parents would leave to work in the fields and return only at dusk. We grew up eating roasted wild tubers, melons, and cucumbers. Here, I foster you by holding you close to my bosom. I am a virgin mother without having delivered a baby," she said, embracing Ammu.

Kaliamma often reprimanded Parothi for throwing palm and coconut leaves into the lake. "One should not pollute the pristine lake. She must be conserved. One should not throw waste into her. She quenches the thirst of one and all."

Ammu would lie with her head on Kaliamma's lap, counting the stars as they sat on the knee-high side wall of the ezhuthupura. She imagined one of the shining stars to be her mother, watching over her. If her mother had survived, Ammu believed that Devayani would have penned verses about those who tried to kill her as well as the plight of the starving Zulus in South Africa. "My mother would've raised her voice and proclaimed to the world that riots spring from the depths of intense pain and anger of men." As she reflected on her mother's brutal death and the tragic way in which her life was cut short and her verses unfinished, Ammu's anger and sorrow found expression in her writing. She would often find herself going numb, her eyes moist with tears.

She felt carefree and childlike with Raju. She would playfully tease him by dipping her legs into the lake and calling out to the *paralmeen*, or tropical fish, to nibble at her toes. "I won't let those fish eat my Kunjava," he would say, pulling her legs out of the water.

Those days and nights were filled with joy for Ammutty, the teenager. She enjoyed treading on the *ooppan*, a grass with sharp spines that grew wild across the kadankunnu. One day, the spines stubbornly stuck to her skirt. When she met Raju, he noticed the prickly grass on her skirt. He made her sit beside him beneath the cashew tree and gently plucked out each spine one by one. "Look at these; they are the shoots of love; that's why they are nicknamed *snehappullu* (love grass). See how much they love me!" Ammu said playfully. "Love shouldn't cause pain to my Kunjava!" Raju retorted.

Suddenly, to their surprise, Kunjammavan, who was supposed to be in Thiruvananthapuram, came darting down the hill, shouting, "Scoundrel! How dare you lift her skirt!" Ammu was stunned into silence, and Raju stood up abruptly.

"Watch what you say, Madhavan Pilla! You're the one who goes under the skirts of many women. The only reason we haven't handled you yet is because you are Ammu's uncle," Raju retorted sharply and swiftly.

Kunjammavan lost his temper and yelled, "I'll break your jaw for this!"

Raju folded up his dhoti, preparing himself for a confrontation. "Madhava, you may try your best," he challenged.

"I will. What will you do?" Kunjammavan countered.

"I haven't pledged my hands to anyone," Raju responded boldly. "I handle oars with this hand. You won't stand a chance," he added in a menacing tone, raising his palm.

"Pookkaithayoor cannot afford to have both of us anymore. It's either you or me. Let me see if I can bury you in this lake," warned Kunjammavan.

He then turned towards Ammu and bellowed, "Go home. Now! You cursed creature! You killed your mother and father just by being born!"

Kunjammavan stormed into the bungalow, swearing and directing his fury towards Kunjikkali. "My father is the only one to blame for this, for allowing all these lowborn scum to live in the *tharavadu* as if they belonged here. You're the one who has supported this girl in all this nonsense. She is hanging around with a converted Pulaya boy. I'll kill you all!" he thundered.

On hearing this, Kunjikkali, who never openly spoke against Kochangunnu, raised her voice.

"Don't insult my clan. We live by working hard. Valiyangunnu made us communists with his actions, but you are trying to undo your father's noble actions. By pretending to be a communist, you're attempting to convert us to non-communists. Do not mistake our silence for fear. Many of us remain silent only because we are thinking of those who sacrificed their lives for us.

"Don't condemn Vaava. She's a sensible girl. I'll chop off any hand that dares to harm her. No mother will ever be a silent witness to any harm wrought upon her child. We survive on the wages we earn through our sweat, each drop containing the salt of our tears," declared Kunjikkali, her authority clear as she held a weeping Ammu close. Kunjammavan winced at seeing a completely different Kunjikkali in all her might for the first time.

Ammu decided she no longer needed Kunjammavan to escort her on her travels to Thiruvananthapuram. She felt capable of managing without her petty uncle's assistance. She anticipated receiving a scholarship based on her exam results, although it would take some time. However, this delay wasn't a concern since Rosamma, who was fairly well-off, had agreed to lend her some money. Now was the opportunity to assert her independence. It was also time to complete the application form for the MA course, a process she expected would take about a week. In the meantime, Kunjammavan left for Thiruvananthapuram with the money from selling coconuts.

Ammu met Raju the next morning. "Were you frightened, Kunjave?" he asked. "He won't do anything. Haven't you heard that barking dogs seldom bite? I would've given him two slaps yesterday, but thought it disrespectful to bash up your uncle. Believe me, I seriously wanted to give him a good smack."

"The certificate is ready. I'll go to Thiruvananthapuram next week. I need to fill out the MA application form and gather my mark lists. The whole process will take about two weeks. But I don't need Kunjammavan to escort me anymore," Ammu said.

"No need at all," Raju endorsed her decision. "We must stand on our own feet. Kunjava should now become Valiyava. Grow like Valiyangunnu and confront hypocrites like Madhavan."

Ammu observed the determination on Raju's face.

The bus from Bhagothimukku was at 9 a.m. Kayalamma Motors, run by Pattukada Viswambharan, was the lifeline connecting the people of Pookkaithayoor to the outside world. Every noon, the bus would reach the junction, park there, and make its return trip the following morning.

Ammu completed her packing the previous night so that she could spend more time with Raju. Early the next morning, she hurried to the lakeshore where he was waiting for her.

"Come quickly, Kunjave. Hop onto the boat; we need to go a bit far," he said, taking her hand and leading her to his boat. "We must head south. There's someone hiding on the southern shore."

The small country boat darted to the southern shore at jet speed. On docking, Raju said, "It's all marshy here. I'll carry you, Kunjave. You can find the hidden one yourself."

Ammu caught a whiff of a familiar fragrance. Behind a cluster of screw pines, she spotted a lone kaitha bloom, its head drooping from the weight. Raju lifted her high with his right hand, holding her close to his chest. With his pocketknife he delicately removed the flower from its stem and offered it to her lovingly, saying, "Here, now you can pluck it." She carefully plucked the bloom, her eyes and nostrils widening to take in its fragrance, as Raju carried her back to the boat.

As the sun rose in the east, its morning rays awakened the tranquil lake from its misty slumber. Ammu smiled, feeling as though she were touched by her lover's presence. They shared some blissful moments together, gliding across the lake in the boat, guided by the southern breeze. Ammu's long, thick hair was flying behind her and Raju tenderly smoothed it down.

"Let's row to the end of the world!" she suggested.

"Wherever we go together will be heaven, Kunjave", he replied warmly.

When the boat reached the shore again, Ammu showed the kaithapoo to her kaitha grove and said, "I had to go to the other shore because you haven't bloomed yet."

Raju lifting Ammu to pluck the kaitha bloom

Raju smiled warmly at her. "You're just like the name I call you, Kunjave. Always innocent like a child, always chatting with flowers."

"But every time I talk to the sun or the moon, I speak only of you," she responded, her face glowing with love.

Suddenly, the gentle breeze gave way to a storm, and the smiling sun was obscured by the clouds. Darkness enveloped the land, and the once serene face of the Mother Lake turned gloomy. Raju gently caressed her wind-tossed hair and held her close. Ammu's lips, now awakened by his touch, ached for the warmth of his kiss. He merely kissed her on her forehead, as the intensity of his passion was cautioned by a wave of pure affection. The fiery desire to be entwined in a deep embrace and the yearning to fuse together were restrained by a profound love that transcended physical yearning.

Moments passed by ... As the wind abated, he began to speak, "Look at the Mother Lake. She has been waiting patiently for a long time. Our day will come, and we must wait until then. I won't ruin it by being hasty. I will protect this virgin chastity until our time, my dream maiden."

As she climbed uphill to head to the bungalow, Ammu wondered, "*Is this charming prince of mine human or divine?*" On returning home, she dropped the kaithapoo in her bag and rushed to catch the Kayalamma Motors bus. She made it just one minute before it departed. From her window seat, she could see Raju on the verandah of the tea shop. Their eyes locked, and they bid adieu, but Ammu could feel her beloved's eyes following her.

Twenty

AMMU NEEDED TO be in Thiruvananthapuram for two weeks, during which she stayed with Sharada teacher in the college hostel. Sharada teacher was packing to return to the UK. She had been pursuing her master's degree in Oxford and had been working part-time there for the past year. However, she had to come back to Kerala to care for her sick mother, who had recently passed away. With her mother gone, Sharada teacher decided to resume her academic career at Oxford. Her best friend-turned-lover, who was also there, had persuaded her to be with him.

"I must leave too, as my man waits for me back home. How long can he continue waiting? We all have our sorrows, just as we all have our dreams," Ammu reflected.

She went to the university to submit her application. Standing amidst the library books, she suddenly sensed Raju's familiar scent—the fragrance of her beloved kaithapoo. Suddenly, she longed to see him. It took her another five days to collect her certificates. During those nights, Raju visited her in dreams, awakening her and whispering the language of love. She would sit in bed, eyes closed and just his face in her mind. She wondered if Raju had begun to haunt her like a spirit. But she was fine with that. In fact, it was what she wanted. She wanted him to be a part of her.

Two weeks later, as she alighted at Bhagothimukku, an ominous stillness hung in the air. She walked to the bungalow and when she reached it, she thought it was strange that Kaliamma was nowhere to be seen. She called out to her. Kaliamma, who was feeding Manikandan, came running to her and took her bag. Her usual welcoming smile was absent; she looked disheartened.

"Oh, Ammu, you're back. Did you collect all your certificates?" Kunjammavan joined them outside, but without his usual arrogance. His voice quavered as he said, "I'll be back," and left abruptly. His demeanour seemed very unusual.

Ammu entered her room and changed out of her travel clothes. Kaliamma brought her a glass of milk. "Vaave... drink this."

"Why milk now?" Ammu asked. "The rice is still cooking, so the meal is not ready yet. You've had a long journey. Drink this," Kaliamma replied.

She drank the milk that Kaliamma offered. After all, it was what her caring foster mother wanted. Kaliamma sat beside her on the bed, took the empty glass from Ammu and placed it on the table.

"I have some terribly sad news for you; it's going to be unbearable for you, my Vaave. But you must know ... Rajumon is gone," Kaliamma said, bursting into tears.

"What? Where? He never said anything about going anywhere," a surprised Ammu said.

"The Mother Lake has taken him. She has drawn him back to her womb," Kaliamma replied, trembling.

"What are you talking about?" Ammu was baffled, tongue-tied and stunned.

"Vaave, we won't see him anymore. He is now formless," Kaliamma broke down inconsolably.

Ammu felt everything around her crumble as she fainted. Kaliamma gently laid an unconscious Ammu on the bed and sprinkled water from the prayer room on her face. She then smeared some holy ash on her forehead. Hours passed by before Ammu slowly regained consciousness. She ran to the lake as though possessed, searching frantically for Raju's boat near the kaitha grove, and screaming his name aloud. "Raju! Raju!" Then, as if possessed, she waded into the water, begging the Mother Lake to take her too. It took all of Kaliamma's strength to pull her out, restrain her and guide her to sit down on the sand.

Ammu collapsed on that sandbar, weeping, crying, screaming, and wailing inconsolably. Kaliamma eventually carried her to the ezhuthupura, to the cot on which Angunnu used to rest.

"I know that you are inconsolable now. But you should know that Raju's boat capsized. No one knows how it happened. There were no witnesses. Kochangunnu was away on a trip, but two of his associates were staying at the farmhouse the day before he left. Kochuraman had arranged their accommodation and meals. The lake was filled with the *choolan eranda* (Indian whistling ducks) huddled together. They covered the entire middle section of the lake. It's a yearly phenomenon. The men likely came here at Kochangunnu's invitation, armed with long rifles to hunt choolan eranda. They had been hunting for some days by then, and Kochuraman had organised a boat from the western shore to carry the shot birds to the toddy shop and get them cooked for the men. Such despicable people! How many more slaughters would it take to satisfy their greed," Kaliamma lamented, her eyes filled with tears.

"The wind carried Raju's boat to Vettikkadavu the day after the men left. It was then that we discovered Raju was missing. His friends from the library set out to look for him, and by the third day, they found his body entangled in our kaitha grove. I took only one look at his lifeless form, just the day before yesterday. Because his body had been in the water for three days, the police advised immediate cremation. It was Kochangunnu who met the police and made all the arrangements."

Ammu was barely conscious by then. "Are you hearing me, Vaave? Paakkaran said they gave Raju a 'red salute' during the cremation. I don't know what that is.

"'Che Raju is not dead; he lives in us,' declared the library crowd, raising slogans in his honour. His parents obeyed Kochangunnu's directives. He is a powerful man with influence in the government. Perhaps the Salvation Army seeks government support as well. I wanted to keep Raju's body until you arrived. I also made the request, but what power do I have? Kochangunnu took charge and swiftly completed all the formalities. Yesterday, he even convened a meeting at Bhagothimukku to mourn Raju's untimely

Raju's vacant boat and the silent choolan eranda

passing. He praised Comrade Raju profusely in his speech. Kunjan Pilla said that he even exhorted the youth to be inspired by Raju," Kaliamma said.

Ammu began to feel faint again. Her nights were haunted by insomnia, and she spent her days staring out at the lake. Every ripple on the water's surface sparked hope that Raju would emerge from its depths. The mornings they had spent together by the lake remained vivid in her memory. "Didn't we make plans to travel together? Why did you go alone and leave me behind?" she kept asking.

"I had asked you what I should bring when I returned. You said you only needed your Kunjava. Your Kunjava is here now, but you left without waiting for me. What should I do now? Where can I meet you again? Please tell me. Speak to me," Ammu begged.

Her tears had dried up. Her thoughts resonated with madness. She felt as though her life had lost its purpose; she felt lifeless and numb. "The time we spent dreaming of a life together was all for nothing; that life has been stolen by time. Why did you suppress our desires? If only you had kissed me deeply, just once, if only we had become one ... But now, what about me? How do I go on without you? Tell me ..." she moaned.

Kaliamma stood silently, listening to Ammu's distraught outpouring. "Write them all down, my dear. Perhaps this is why you've learnt to express yourself. Just like I use a broom, an axe and a machete, doesn't Vaava wield a pen as a weapon?" And so Ammu began to spend her nights scribbling down the thoughts of her rambling mind, which extended into the days. Words became her only solace.

"I must continue my studies. Pookkaithayoor has nothing to offer but pain. It awakens death," Ammu resolved. The thought of leaving Manthoppu began to haunt her. However, Kaliamma encouraged her. "You must leave this place for a while. Kaliamma will take care of everything here."

During this time, Kunjammavan became an occasional visitor. He found it difficult to look Ammu in the eyes, as if harbouring a secret. Ammu couldn't bear to look at him either, convinced that Raju's boat wouldn't have sunk in a storm on its own. Raju was a skilled boatman and an excellent swimmer. What had happened was definitely betrayal and murder.

"Those monsters didn't miss their mark. Raju would never go near those birds. He had always stood for their conservation, saying that they were migratory birds and shouldn't be disturbed or shot for meat. But this was murder. They aimed at and shot the person who opposed the slaughter of those birds," Ammu said, and then cautioned Kaliamma, "They'll target you next. Be careful."

"You leave this place, Vaave. I am sharpening my blade to finish them off," Kaliamma reassured Ammu.

Twenty-one

AMMU WASN'T SURE where to escape. It was then that she received a letter from Sharada teacher in Oxford.

"Come. You can do your master's here. After that, we can register you for a D.Phil. Classes start in October, after Michaelmas. So, get your certificates, secure a nomination for the Commonwealth Scholarship from the university and come to Oxford," the letter said.

That settled her dilemma. Rosamma's uncle owned a travel agency in Thiruvananthapuram, so she arranged for Ammu's air tickets and travel to Oxford. They had shared a room for three years as close friends and confidantes, and such friendships often run deeper than blood relations.

Ammu didn't ask Kunjammavan for money. She didn't even want to talk to him because she was filled with hatred and disgust for the man. What shocked her the most was his cruelty to his mother, who had loved him blindly. Ammu was often witness to Ammamma using astrologer Kittan Jolsyan's predictions to reject the matrimonial alliances that came for her beloved son. Kittan would cite several issues with the horoscopes of the proposed girls, such as lacking heavenly blessings or having a *Chovva Dosham* (the planet Mars in an unfavourable position), *Rajju Dosham* or other marital problems.

When Ammamma rejected a girl due to her dark complexion from exposure to the sun while selling coconut leaves, fronds, and stalks, Ammutty couldn't help but wonder if that woman was as beautiful as her Kaliamma.

"What is wrong with a dark complexion? Is it only a fair complexion that makes one beautiful? Isn't Raju, with his tanned skin, the most handsome man I have ever met in life," Ammu would ask herself such questions.

Both mother and son had their reasons for rejecting marriage proposals. Ammamma was reluctant to marry off her son, being too selfish and possessive to accept another woman in his life. On the other hand, Kunjammavan had a secret, unbreakable bond with a girl, quite unacceptable to his mother, ever since his college days. That was his secret affair at Neyyattinkara in Thiruvananthapuram. Radhamoni Thankachi, the granddaughter of a distant relative of his mother, was his sweetheart.

Ammamma had sent Kunjammavan to Neyyattinkara to reclaim their lost possessions. The young girl, adept at seduction, kept Kunjammavan under her spell. What would Ammamma have done if she had found out about this? She would've locked herself in the cellar until her death! Kunjammavan was clever enough to hide his affair from his devoted mother and refrained from bringing his beloved to Manthoppu until Ammamma's first *Aandu Bali* (death anniversary rituals).

Death had forever robbed Ammu and Pookkaithayoor of the sweet fragrance of the kaithapoo. For Ammu, the flower now carried the scent of death and unbearable loss—first, her beloved mother, and now, Raju. Desperate to escape both the fragrance and the memories of the land, she expedited all the arrangements necessary for her travel.

Ammu arrived in London in early September. Sharada teacher's empathetic presence was a source of solace. However, even in England, Ammu's thoughts frequently drifted to that tiny boat, rowing across the lake with Raju.

Kunjikkali handed over all the savings she had kept hidden from the prying eyes of Kochuraman to Vaava for her travel expenses. The two of them could barely hold back their tears at the time of departure. Ammu left with teary eyes, promising to return upon receiving the scholarship money. "I'll see you soon," she promised. "I will not cry. I'll wait for you," Kunjikkali replied. Ammu noticed determination in her Kaliamma's eyes, as though she were preparing for something.

A year later, Ammu found out what Kunjikkali had been preparing for. She was stupefied when she received Khalasi Paakkaran's letter: "Kunjikkali gave birth to a child out of wedlock. Kunjammavan has kicked her out of the bungalow. He has also barred her from the ezhuthupura. She gave birth in the shack on the slope, with no one to help. We saw her at the evening market with the infant in her arms, buying rice, tamarind and ten pieces of dried red chili with money she earned by selling cashew nuts. I offered her some money, but she refused, saying, 'Leave me alone, Paakkara. I am a bad woman now. I have given birth to a bastard. I was wronged by those who called me barren. I wanted to prove that I was not

Kunjikkali parading before Kochuraman with her baby

barren. You blame a woman for not bearing a child and then condemn her for bearing one. Is it fair?' She spoke loudly, as if she had gone mad.

"Kochuraman was distilling *koda* in the paddy field in Shappumukku. She paraded the child in front of him, challenging him openly. He sat with his eyes downcast, speechless. 'I am waiting for my son to grow up, and then I'll train him to pound the scum who, after marrying his mother, carried someone else's children without shame, challenging her womanhood,' she threatened Kochuraman.

"I've written at length to let you know, Ammu, that you are needed here as soon as possible," Paakkaran concluded.

Ammu was deeply troubled. "*Can Kaliamma do any wrong? It's unbelievable to hear such things about someone as pure as the pristine springs of the Mother Lake. But there are moments when even the lake becomes turbulent, unsettled, and polluted. Did Kunjikkali, too, become ordinary in such a moment of turmoil? Even if that is the case, who am I to prosecute or judge Kaliamma,*" she reflected.

"*Haven't I, too, intensely craved to become one with Raju in those moments of fiery passion? It was Raju who controlled this impulse with his self-restraint. It was his affectionate concern for his Kunjava and for our future. But it was all in vain. There is only one certainty in life: living in the moment. And Kaliamma, who knows everything, would undoubtedly be aware of the value of such moments. She would never be wrong or do wrong. Society passes verdicts without considering what may be a precious truth for an individual. Who could have caused such* turmoil in Kaliamma? Could it be that someone forced himself on her?"Ammu wondered.

"*I must hear it from her. But I can't go home without completing the course here.*" So the questions remained an enigma, haunting Ammu.

The classes in Oxford were uplifting, filled with enriching interactive sessions and libraries that housed mountains of knowledge. She scaled each book like Mount Everest and found the experience challenging yet incredibly gratifying. She felt as though some books were meant for Raju when she came across the many names and quotes she had first heard from him. For someone who had only seen the world through books from a corner in Pookkaithayoor, Raju's insights evoked in her an ecstatic joy mixed with pain. The emptiness she felt was unfathomable. At night, she would whisper and cry, "I miss you, Raju", as she clutched her pillow and held it close to her chest. Though Sharada was a faculty member at the community college, they always caught up every weekend. That was Ammu's only source of comfort and relief. She could only complete her master's course because of Sharada teacher's guidance and support.

Ammu remained unsettled and restless after learning about Kaliamma's situation and was eager to return and meet her. But she had to settle her debts, and her meagre savings were not sufficient for a return air ticket.

It was five years after Ammu had first arrived in England that she finally returned home. She found her homeland drastically changed. Now, there were more houses, roads, vehicles and people. She reached Pookkaithayoor by evening. Manthoppu looked like a haunted house, completely abandoned. Not even the mango trees showed faint signs of blooming.

As Kali had mentioned earlier, Kunjammavan now lived with his wife in her ancestral home. Ammu went to the ezhuthupura and found it all tidied up. In the courtyard, a three-year-old boy played with a toy bullock cart made with wheels from tender coconuts. It was a curious sight. On seeing a stranger, he ran down, calling for his mother. Kaliamma, who was sweeping dead leaves, hurried over but hesitated at offering a warm embrace. She had changed and now resembled a warrior, moving from one warfront to another. Kunjuneelandan, the toddler, ran to his mother, hiding behind her *kaili*, an informal dhoti.

"Kaliamma, why do you stand so far away from your Vaava? Don't you want your daughter anymore because you now have a son to pamper?"Ammu grumbled. Kaliamma cried out to her Vaava with uncontrollable tears that contained a lifetime of suppressed pain and fury. Her wail sounded like the existential anguish of a lonesome woman. It spoke of the battles she had fought alone—the battles she had resumed from ground zero, unarmed! It all broke loose and descended like an avalanche. Ammu joined in her pain and it took a while for the tide of despair to abate.

When Kunjuneelandan came crying for milk, Kaliamma lovingly nursed him. She cradled him in her lap and let him suckle at her breasts until he was satiated. When Ammu expressed her hunger, Kaliamma quickly prepared a snack of roasted tubers and *kanthari* chutney and served it to her along with black coffee.

"Kochangunnu left yesterday. He won't let me enter the house. The keys are with him. He left me with these keys when Paakkaran informed him of your arrival today," Kali said. Ammu took some chocolates from her bag and offered them to Kunjuneelandan. And when she asked about Kochuraman, Kaliamma started narrating his story.

Twenty-two

KUNJAMMAVAN AND HIS wife, Radhamoni Thankachi, moved into Manthoppu Bungalow, taking full control of their affairs. They made the controversial decision to sell the Aayirappara Kandam, which left the dependent workers destitute. Kochuraman, accompanied by Vasanthi and her new boyfriend, Rowdy Paachan, arrived to evict Kunjikkali from her hut in the valley. Paachan posed himself as a tough thug skilled in wrestling and other forms of fighting. However, the visionary Valiyangunnu had included Kunjikkali's name in the title deed.

"This piece of land was given to me by Manthoppilangunnu, and I intend to live here with my child until my last breath," Kunjikkali said, standing her ground.

"But Angunnu never intended for you to live here with your illegitimate son. If he were here today, he himself would've banished you from this land," Kochuraman retorted.

"Well, it's your own impotence that has led to this situation, you Kannali," Kunjikkali shot back, gripping her machete. Kochuraman's tongue froze in response to Kali's sharp retort. Even Rowdy Paachan took a step back. Fearing for their lives, they strategically withdrew and were forced to flee by Kali's unbridled fury.

Vasanthi relocated Kochuraman to her outer shed, where she kept her hidden stash of alcohol, citing his intolerable coughing and wheezing. In a drunken brawl at the toddy shop, during which a few men were hacked and some were stabbed, Kochuraman's lame leg suffered further injuries. The police arrested him, but no one bailed him out. Eventually, the charges were dropped and he was released.

A few days later, news surfaced of Kochuraman's body being found in the sewage by the canal road near the toddy shop. Milkmaid Dakshayani, known as Pookkaithayoor's unofficial news broadcaster, later reported that Rowdy Paachan had severely beaten Kochuraman for attempting to pilfer booze at night, and he was deserted by all. Villagers discovered his body being consumed by ants in the sewer. Dakshayani shared this grim information with Kunjikkali when they met at the evening market.

"The ants are going to eat up your *pulayan* (husband). There's no one to bury him," Dakshayani said.

"Look at my neck. Do you see a sacred thread there? I broke it off a long time ago and threw it at him. He is not my pulayan," Kunjikkali retorted.

Though she did not have any feelings of concern for Kochuraman, Kunjikkali was troubled by the impact on Manthoppilangunnu's esteemed reputation. If Angunnu were alive, not even a stranger's body would be left for the ants to feast upon. Kali remained loyal to her master even years after his death and sought to uphold his noble traditions.

That night, Kunjikkali went to the barn carrying some cattle feed for the poorly nourished Manikandan. She offered the feed to the unfed ox and then proceeded to oil the rusty wheels of his cart before hitching him to it. Lighting a kerosene lantern and hanging it in front of the cart, she climbed aboard and said, "Manikanda, we must go to a nearby place."

Manikandan had a unique understanding of Kaliamma, far better than other humans did, and he obeyed her. Grateful to her for keeping him alive with regular feedings of grass and water, Manikandan moved forward as directed.

The world around them lay shrouded in the deep slumber of the night as the cart rolled past Shappumukku. There, in a trench formed by water seeping from the country road, lay a lifeless body covered only in a towel, swarmed by ants. Holding her breath and masking her nose, Kunjikkali used a *kaili* to cover the corpse before carrying it to the cart. Manikandan pulled the cart slowly towards her, as if understanding the task at hand. For Kali, the company of cattle provided more comfort than that of people.

Manikandan, who knew the path well, paused on a side road leading to the bungalow. "Proceed gently down the slope as far as the cart can go," she instructed him. Manikandan came to a stop when the road reached a downward slope. Kunjikkali disembarked and carried the corpse to the north of her shanty. Calculating a fair distance from the lake because she didn't want to pollute the holy lake, she took a shovel and vigorously began digging into the earth. Afterwards, she buried the body in a shallow grave.

The next day, Dakshayani informed that Kochuraman's body had vanished from the drain. How could ants consume

Kunjikkali digging a grave at midnight to bury Kochuraman

an entire human body? The people of Pookkaithayoor were dumbstruck.

By the time Kali finished talking about her mysterious assignment, it was well past midnight. Ammu glanced at Kunjuneelandan, who was sound asleep, wondering whether Kali would disclose another secret story about his birth.

"The Mother Lake was the only witness. Now, you too know, Kunjave. I fulfilled my duty," Kaliamma said, sighing with relief.

Awestruck, Ammu gazed at Kaliamma as she recounted how she had carried and buried Kochuraman's decaying corpse—the man she despised and once contemplated killing.

"*Is she a woman of flesh and blood or an angel? How could she forgive the man who destroyed her life?*" Kaliamma had become a puzzle to Ammu. The affectionate woman who had raised her had transformed into an enigma, as unfathomable as the lake itself.

The three-year-old who darted around the ezhuthupura was another mystery. Clutching a fistful of candies, he asked for more, his mouth smeared with exotic chocolate. He ran around with a young, tender coconut affixed to the midrib of a coconut leaf blade. Was he another one of Kaliamma's secret miracles? "Tell me the truth, Kaliamma. Did you really give birth to him?"Ammu asked pointedly.

"Vaave, it's as real as this lake. I gave birth to him. Look at these scratch marks on my belly. I did this to myself when I couldn't bear the labour pains. I had to prove to everyone who called me barren that they were mistaken. I wanted everyone to know that Kali, who became a foster mother at the age of seven, could give birth to a son.

"I know you haven't asked about his father. He's a truck driver who delivered food supplies from Tenkasi to Viswambharan's store. We used to cross paths while going to bathe at the ghat. Gradually, he started coming to the shack to meet me. He would ask for water to drink and fire to light his *beedi*. He's a strong man.

"If you ask me if he is a good man, I no longer know who is good and who is not. I once knew good people. Kumaran Mash lived in our hut when I was nine or ten. He told me good stories and showered me with great affection, more than my *Achan* (father) did. When he found out his comrades were being beaten and interrogated for Kumaran's whereabouts, and when he learnt that one of his closest friends was lynched to death for not revealing his location, he left his safe hideout. He said he would surrender to the police after seeing his departed comrade one last time. He told me about his friend, a comrade, who took only one rupee as a donation for the party fund when he was offered five rupees.

"And there was Manthoppilangunnu, who, like King Maveli, didn't know deceit or betrayal. He once gave a new lease of life to an orphan boy who was ungrateful to him.

"Then there was my Rajumon, who started earning his bread right from his early teenage days. He opened a library and collected books for youth who couldn't afford to buy them. He always took care of you like his Kunjava, ensuring not a single scratch marred you. He tried to educate the lowborn working class of the land. They were all exceptional men, but not the truck driver. He was merely a potent male."

Kali stopped briefly before continuing, "Kunjikkali desired just one night with a man. I also wanted to find out for myself if I was barren. I knew I wasn't when my menstrual cycle stopped. From then on, I endured all the discomfort in my womb, only to give birth to a child. I didn't need anyone's support for childbirth. I only desired that seed to be sown." She sounded bold, so sure of herself.

"The truck driver, who left the next day, never returned to see me. He must have heard the village gossip about my pregnancy out of wedlock. That put an end to his visits to the ghat. All I ever desired was one night with a man. I had no wish to see him again. Giving birth to a baby was all that mattered to me. Nursing him and hearing him call me 'Amma' was all I ever wanted. Now no scoundrel will bother me, asking to 'keep me company' at night. They all think being a woman means silently tolerating all torture without raising a voice. Even my mother taught me this as a child. But I began to raise my voice.

"It was Kumaran Mash who empowered me by opening a window to the world for me. I didn't simply protest with words; I showed it through my actions too. One afternoon, after Kumaran Mash had left, Chanthiran, who collected wild honey, came to our dwelling. Kochucherukkan was asleep at that time. Usually, Achan would barter rice for honey. This time, when Chanthiran offered to pour the honey straight into my mouth, I opened my mouth with great zeal. But he inserted his penis into my mouth with a perverse smile.

I didn't hesitate to bite! My teeth dug deep into it. He ran away screaming in pain. My teeth were sharp then, and they still are now. But I don't need my teeth anymore because I have this machete. I didn't even tell my mother about it and remained silent for a long time. I was furious. In those days, low-caste people like us wouldn't speak out about such things out of fear. But we should. We should bellow loudly for the entire world to hear. Only then will we scare such perverts away."

"Vaave, you've matured and seen the world. You have a way with words. Speak and write for those who are voiceless and oppressed. The world will heed Ammu Devu Pilla. That's all Kaliamma wants."

Ammu noticed the glimmer of hope in Kali's eyes.

Twenty-three

KUNJAMMAVAN CAME BACK to Pookkaithayoor on the third day after Ammu arrived. "Your aunt had reached the end of her first trimester, but it ended in abortion, just like the last one," he said, his face veiled in despair.

"Your aunt is not comfortable living here. In Neyyattinkara, she has her mother, sister, and several maids to attend to her needs. Besides, she does not appreciate Kali living here. It's a shame for honourable families like ours to host a disgraced woman like her," he added.

Ammu felt tempted to question whether his own actions reflected those of someone from an honourable family. But she chose not to confront him at that moment.

"We have decided to sell all our properties here and build a bungalow on your aunt's share of land in Maruthur, Neyyattinkara," Kunjammavan said. Ammu was relieved that he had finally revealed his cards.

"In that case, you should re-register the kadankunnu that Valiyachan gave me. I want to pay the taxes as the land's owner. I also plan to continue my studies," Ammu, too, disclosed her plans.

"You can continue your studies, but according to the

provision, to become the independent owner of the land, you must get married," Kunjammavan pointed out.

"I intend to pursue research, so family life is not possible now. I have no plans to marry at this time," Ammu made her stance clear.

Kunjammavan hastily left for Thiruvananthapuram, after telling her reluctance to marry meant she didn't need the property either.

Ammu informed Kaliamma of the recent developments. "He's being obstinate. They are the greedy lot who have robbed the properties of Manthoppilamma. I understand your feelings, but this situation is a trap. You should escape, embitter and adapt your mind if necessary. Conceal your goodness to survive in this world. Sometimes, a bit of cunning is needed," Kaliamma advised Ammu.

Ammu was torn about what to do next. Once she registered for a DPhil, it could take years to complete. Kunjikkali would suffer without shelter and income, and now she had a child to care for. The piece of land given to her by Valiyangunnu had a joint title with Kochuraman, who had pledged it to Vattavila Vasanthi, and it was now plagued by rowdy troublemakers.

Kaliamma had built a chambalpura on the *purampokku* (government land) on the slope of the kadankunnu to collect ash, using green coconut leaves, leaf stalks, and strong tuber stems. She burned dry leaves nearby and later stored the ashes in her chambalpura to keep them away dry. She earned a living by selling the ashes to boatmen. In the corner of her chambalpura, she prepared rice gruel, and at night, she slept on the verandah of the ezhuthupura, telling stories to Neelandan while stray dogs kept her company.

"My Kaliamma should not continue to suffer such a life. If getting married can prevent it, then so be it," Ammu finally decided.

"I have decided to accept Kunjammavan's conditions. But Raju will continue to live deep in my heart. I don't care who Kunjammavan brings as my suitor. I will sign on the marriage register, and Kunjammavan must sign over control of my shares to me," Ammu told Kaliamma.

"Vaave, you should never make such a decision for my sake. I'll leave this place with my son. I just don't want those greedy mongrels to usurp what Manthoppilangunnu gave you," Kaliamma replied.

"How can I ever sleep peacefully in a room, on a bed, while you sleep on a verandah? How can I eat knowing this mother who fed me is starving?" Both mother and daughter cried out in anguish, and yet their pain remained with them.

Kunjammavan didn't expect Ammu to agree to marriage, but he feigned searching for suitors for her. In the course of his apparent search, one Raghuraman Menon from Ottapalam emerged as a promising match for Ammu. He was a professor of psychology at Leicester University in England and inclined towards settling abroad. He seldom visited his homeland, so he was unlikely to demand Ammu's share of the property. Kunjammavan considered all these factors with his characteristic cunning.

When Raghuraman arrived to meet Ammu, dressed and speaking like an Englishman, his appearance failed to fully convince. When he invited Ammu out for a stroll, she assumed it was to admire the lake. So she mentally prepared to extol the beauty and virtues of the lake in Pookkaithayoor, drawing comparisons to the lakes of the Lake District. To her disappointment, Raghuraman's questions were about coconut toddy tapping. *"Well, he's from Palakkad, so it's hardly surprising as toddy tapping is common there,"* she reasoned with herself.

The conversation then shifted to foreign liquor brands, and Ammu soon realised she was talking to an alcoholic. She thought the marriage might work to her advantage, as he would be inebriated all the time and leave her alone. But she decided to be honest anyway. *"I must tell him about myself. I cannot betray his trust,"* Ammu convinced herself. She openly discussed her brief yet passionate affair with Raju and talked about their deep love and commitment to each other. "My body and mind still belong to him even though he is gone," she confessed, almost on the verge of breaking down.

Raghuraman's reaction, however, was unexpected—a mocking laughter. "These silly girls ... nurturing high ideals and platonic affairs. I pity them. They live in their dreams, forgetting to enjoy their bodies. I do not care at all about this nonsense," he scoffed. Ammu was stunned by his insensitive response.

"This man seems to belong to an entirely different genus—a psychologist who fails to grasp the intricacies of the mind! I don't care how big a unicorn he thinks he is; this is my way out of Kunjammavan's deceitful plans," Ammu decided.

With Ammu consenting to the marriage, Comrade Madhavan had no choice but to proceed with the wedding.

"I prefer to have a registered civil wedding. I don't want any ceremonies or celebrations in this horrible house of death," Ammu stated firmly.

Kunjammavan breathed a sigh of relief, realising he had just spared himself the huge expenses of a wedding venue, a lavish wedding feast and other arrangements.

Ammu's next statement brought even further relief. "I don't want any gold either."

Her aunt, Radhamoni, was the happiest to hear this. Her eyes gleamed at the prospect of becoming the sole owner of all those precious traditional gold ornaments that once belonged to Manthoppilamma and were now locked in her cabinet. She had been eyeing them for a long time.

"But, my dear, you must wear some jewellery on your ears, neck and arms. Otherwise, it would look awkward." It was the first time her aunt showed concern and kindness towards her. Ammu smirked at the hypocrisy.

"Don't push her if she's not interested. It's the trend these days to wear minimal jewellery," Kunjammavan interjected.

"It's not about following trends or style. Inspired by Gandhiji, my mother donated her gold to the poor. I'm simply following in her footsteps," Ammu said, certain of her words and decision.

"Why do you want to hurt the feelings of a poor, motherless child?" This time, it was her aunt who sided with Ammu in the conversation.

Raghuraman also agreed to the arrangement. For him, this marriage was merely a gesture to appease his elderly parents. Only five people from the groom's side, including his uncle and aunt, and representatives from the *Karayogam*,* participated in the wedding ceremony. On the bride's side were Kunjammavan, Radhamoni Thankachi, her elder sister Devaki Thankachi, Pattupadi Viswambharan and his daughter, Lalitha, Ammu's close childhood friend.

The bride, Ammu Devu Pilla, wore a brand new handloom saree, bud-shaped stone earrings, and a black-beaded necklace. Lalitha Chechi's eyes welled up at seeing the bride without any ornaments. Meanwhile, the bride's aunt glowed like a newly-wed in a rich silk saree and all the gold jewellery that once belonged to Ammamma. Kunjammavan explained to the people of Pookkaithayoor that he was simply honouring Ammu's wishes for a modest wedding.

As the wedding party prepared to leave for Ottapalam, Kaliamma held Ammu close, kissed her forehead and said, "Be bold and strong, Vaave. Kayalamma (Mother Lake) and Angunnu's soul will always protect you."

Ammu got into the car, composing herself and dabbing her moist eyes with the edge of her saree. Raghuraman was already seated in the front. It was midnight when they reached Ottapalam, Raghuraman's native place in Malabar. It was an old *tharavadu*, and his parents were innocent village folk. Raghuraman's mother, who welcomed the bride into the family home with a lit lamp, appeared weary. Raghuraman

---

* The local units of Hindu Nairs

Ammu signing the marriage register

had instructed them beforehand to keep the rituals simple. He didn't even touch the glass of sweet milk meant to be shared by the newly-weds on their first night; Ammu drank it all herself.

"Ammu, you can sleep. I have some work to do," Raghuraman said before heading to the adjacent room. Ammu felt relieved and soon drifted off to sleep.

Ammu loved the calm atmosphere of her in-laws' home. They lived amidst lush green paddy fields and a pond filled with water lilies. People from the neighbourhood dropped in to meet the new daughter-in-law of Puthethu Tharavadu. Raghuraman's parents were ecstatic; this was all he had hoped for from this marriage. As expected by Raju's beloved Kunjava, nothing disturbing took place during this time.

It took another two months for the kadankunnu to be formally transferred to Ammu's name. Raghuraman hastily returned to England, leaving Ammu behind at Manthoppu. He couldn't extend his leave any longer, so he allowed Ammu to join him later. Ammu welcomed this arrangement, as it meant that she could spend some more time with Kaliamma and play with and pamper little Neelandan. Yet, amidst these fleeting moments of happiness, the eternal agony of separation haunted her. In times of deep distress, she longed for Raju's comforting touch.

"I fall upon the thorns of life; I bleed. Why don't you come to wipe off the blood as you did in our first encounter," Ammu lamented. Momentarily forgetting reality, she waited for his response, hoping he would ascend from the depths of the Mother Lake upon hearing her quote Shelley and deliver a speech in his revolutionary ardour. But it was all in vain.

"Where have you hidden my Raju, oh, Mother Lake? Show him to me once, just once. Let me embrace him and bid him goodbye one last time. You can take him back after that. Look around; can't you see all the kaitha being destroyed? There's no fragrance left in the air anymore." Ammu spent a lot of time crying, complaining, and then falling silent, followed by lengthy monologues.

Kaliamma would let her purge herself of the intense, irreparable grief by wailing aloud by the lakeshore before taking her back home. She repeatedly reminded Ammu, "Vaave, you should not give up. You must reach your goal. Rajumon will be happy to see that happen."

However, there were times when even Kaliamma would lose her stoic composure and break into deep wails. Yet, she always managed to regain her composure quickly.

"I will slay those who come to destroy our kaitha in the name of Kochangunnu. Where they once slashed, there are now sprouts," she declared.

Kunjammavan left, pretending to be relieved, after handing over the deed for the kadankunnu to Ammu. But she found true relief only when she finally handed over the key to the ezhuthupura to Kaliamma.

"From now on, my mother is not homeless. I will return after completing what I've begun," Ammu said before proceeding on her journey. Kaliamma's visage glowed for a moment. She kissed Ammu's forehead and hugged her tightly.

"Let this kiss remain until your return. You will never fail; victory is yours. Until then, I will protect Mother Lake and her children," Kaliamma proclaimed with new-found strength while holding Neelandan close. Ammu felt at peace knowing that Kaliamma was not alone.

Twenty-four

RAGHURAMAN WAS A faculty member in the renowned psychology department at Leicester University. "We have a single-family home. You can reach here from the airport by train. I'll be waiting for you at the station," he had written to Ammu in a letter. Ammu travelled as per his instructions. When she arrived, they exchanged cordial "hellos" like acquaintances and spoke about the weather. It was twilight when they finally reached home.

After a while, Raghuraman stepped out, apparently for a meeting. When he returned, Ammu was half asleep due to the jet lag. He introduced her to a blue-eyed, bald-headed man he had brought home with him. "Meet my best friend, Charles Rogers," he said, before leading him to the study upstairs.

It soon became clear to Ammu that Mr Rogers was a regular presence in their home, often staying there. The house had a kitchenette and a spacious balcony upstairs. When Raghuraman confessed that Charlie was not just a friend but also his romantic partner, with whom he shared an unbreakable bond, Ammu finally understood his indifference towards her.

She didn't object to his sexuality and was aware that

homosexuality might have underlying genetic and biological causes. However, she questioned why such a man should marry a woman. When Ammu raised this question, Raghuraman admitted that he had done so to give in to his parents' expectations that he would marry.

"Both of us are fulfilling this marriage to placate our families and those around us. But you're free to lead your own life, just as I will live mine," Raghuraman said.

Ammu agreed that such an arrangement was in their best interests—two human beings living under the same roof, akin to sharing accommodations in a lodge. The Sexual Offences Act of 1967 decriminalised private homosexual acts between two men over the age of 21 in England and Wales. Gay bars were active in big cities like Manchester and Birmingham, which Raghuraman and his partner Charlie frequented.

"You may join us if you wish. You can wear my jeans and a top," Raghuraman said, extending an invitation to his "wife". However, the visible anger and contempt on Ammu's face made him turn to Charlie and pass a mocking comment, "Silly dreamer who insists on wasting her life!"

"This world also belongs to those who live for their minds rather than just gratifying their bodies. This is what sets us apart from animals," Ammu brooded.

Ammu didn't need to think too much to choose a topic for her DPhil thesis: 'Gender Politics and Racism of the 1970s as Discussed in Maya Angelou's book, *I Know Why the Caged Bird Sings*.' Ammu understood why a caged bird continued to sing. The unhealed scars of the Durban riots, apartheid, racism, and the untouchability, oppression and segregation

Ammu at the University Library in England

suffered by Kunjikkali's caste—all were burning experiences that had made her empathetic to the pain of others. She could deeply resonate with Angelou's poignant autobiographical account.

An eight-year-old African American girl, who was raped by her mother's boyfriend, confided in a family member about her trauma. Later, she discovered that her assailant had been killed. Overwhelmed with guilt, she believed she was responsible for his death, convinced that her voice had somehow caused it. This belief silenced her for the next five years. However, a teacher came into her life—someone as tender as pomegranate blooms. Mrs Flowers, through her compassion and care, influenced and helped the young girl, Maya, in finding her voice. This new-found voice later manifested through her memoirs and poetry, like precious pearls.

What topic could resonate more with someone who has been scorched by the flares of life's experiences? Over the years, Ammu faced many transformative experiences. Her supervisor, Dr Richardson, was a compassionate intellectual. While he was both graceful and sombre, his guidance was never coercive. Research never felt like a task or a tiring experience for Ammu. When Sharada teacher moved to Canada after her marriage, Ammu further immersed herself in books to compensate for that void. Now that she had to travel between Leicester and Oxford, she did her research part-time.

Occasional letters from Khalasi Paakkaran, who continued to maintain with Ammu the friendship he once shared with

Raju, were her only link to home. Paakkaran would update her on significant events, such as Kunjammavan selling Manthoppu Bungalow and estate and moving to his new bungalow at Maruthur.

Later, she received news of Kunjammavan stopping his travels after being diagnosed with Alzheimer's disease. Paakkaran visited him once, but when he looked in through the window, Kunjammavan didn't recognise him. Radhamoni Thankachi informed Paakkaran that Kunjammavan had grown averse to bathing and had become aggressive, attacking those who came close. Hence, he was locked in his room. Ammu believed his fate was befitting. After all, he had done many things that were best forgotten. Perhaps, Alzheimer's, she mused, was a godsend for him.

Meanwhile, Kaliamma had enrolled Neelandan in the Achyutha Vilasam School. He was now in Class IV. Every day, he would leave the house with a slate, books, and a packed lunch, ostensibly for school, but instead, he would hang around outside Viswambharan's store, looking at the *pandi lorries* (trucks from Tamil Nadu) unloading stock.

Kaliamma hurried to the store when Dakshayani informed her that her son was playing truant from school. On seeing him assisting with unloading goods, she initially slapped him. Then, she gathered him up in her arms, weeping, and took him back to the kadankunnu, soothing his pain with kisses. "Even though he's illegitimate, she loves that child with all her heart," Paakkaran had commented in his letter.

The next letter brought tragic news. Neelandan had disappeared. Where would a child, barely ten, go? Was he abducted by child traffickers? Kaliamma left no stone unturned on the kadankunnu, crying aloud and calling out to her Mother Lake. When she eventually arrived at Viswambharan's store in her quest, the assistant informed her that Neelandan had left with the lorry driver. Devastated, Kaliamma began rambling like a lunatic. It was Dakshayani who helped her back to the kadankunnu.

"Can pumpkin seeds grow into melons?"Paakkaran quipped. Ammu didn't like his remark and yearned to return home. She desired to go back to Kaliamma, but Jessy, her friend and fellow student, discouraged her.

"I'm going home after three months, so I'll meet Kaliamma then and spend a day with her. You should focus on completing your thesis ... It's nearly done, and it wouldn't be right to leave it unfinished. After 60,000 words, stopping now would make things difficult later. Wait for another three months," Jessy advised Ammu.

Jessy visited her home in Thrissur at least twice a year for *Ambu Perunal* (the church festival) and her father's death anniversary. Her family's jewellery business had a branch in Kollam. So, every time Jessy went home, Ammu would send money for Kaliamma and chocolates for Neelandan with her. Jessy would then go to Manthoppu to meet Kaliamma, who would send banana chips and *arimurukku* for Ammu. Jessy couldn't go home the previous time due to illness. She eventually left three months later, and this time, Ammu anxiously awaited her return.

Twenty-five

AMMU CALLED JESSY the very morning she returned from India, but Jessy sounded reluctant to speak over the phone. Instead, she invited Ammu over to her place so they could talk in detail. Without hesitation, Ammu gathered her essentials and headed to Jessy's place. She saw no reason to call or wait for her husband, Raghuraman, who often returned home late in the night or not at all, enjoying his social outings with friends. With his spare key, he'd let himself in, crash into bed and wake up late to prepare for his next day. He thoroughly enjoyed his carefree lifestyle. Ammu wasn't overly concerned about him; her focus was on reaching the railway station quickly. She sprinted with her backpack to catch the 2.30 p.m. train, and for once, British Rail was on time!

It was late in the evening by the time she arrived at Jessy's home. The lifeless smile that greeted Ammu immediately sparked anxiety within her. Quickly hanging her coat on the door hanger, she wasted no time with pleasantries and asked urgently, "Did you not meet Kaliamma? What are you hiding from me?"

"I'll tell you. But first, have this cup of hot coffee and warm yourself up," Jessy responded, turning on the coffee maker and staring at the boiling water.

"Jessy, please spare me this anxiety and frankly tell me what happened," Ammu pressed, interrupting her friend's focus on making coffee.

"I couldn't meet Kaliamma. I went to the ezhuthupura, but she wasn't there. It looked abandoned, like no one had been there for a while. I searched all over the kadankunnu and along the lakeshore. I even sent driver Lonappan to the junction to enquire about her. People mentioned a fire that occurred about a month ago, which destroyed the chambalpura and its surroundings. Since no one lived nearby, the fire went unnoticed until fishermen spotted the smoke the next morning. There's nothing left," Jessy explained solemnly.

Ammu didn't have the strength to listen to the whole incident. "What tragedy has befallen Kaliamma, who raised me as her own from a very young age? She fed and clothed me, and here I am in a foreign land, living in comfort, pursuing a doctorate. How selfish I am!" Ammu cursed herself.

Unable to delay any longer, she made a decision. That night, she booked a ticket home on a flight that departed at 10 a.m. the following day. She stayed with Jessy that night. Before leaving for the airport, Ammu called Raghuraman from Jessy's phone and said, "Raghu, I am leaving for Kerala. Something terrible has happened to Kaliamma. Jessy went to the ezhuthupura to meet her, but she was missing ..."

She ignored Raghu's irritating questions about who Kaliamma was to her and immediately ended the call. "Those who don't understand the bond between Kaliamma and me certainly do not know me either. It's better not to talk to such people," she decided.

Ammu arrived in Thiruvananthapuram early the next morning and hired a taxi to Pookkaithayoor. Thickets now covered the place where the Manthoppu Bungalow had once proudly stood, their height nearly matching that of a grown man. With a heavy heart, she whispered to herself, "*Goodbye, my love.*" Only the grand well remained on the east side of the once-vibrant estate. Following the overgrown path to the kadankunnu, the city driver had a tough time manoeuvring through the wild cacti and *konna* (Indian Laburnum) lining the road. Ammu paid the taxi fare and sent the driver on his way, opting to walk through the familiar path alone. Memories flooded back as she recalled the days when she strolled that route with Kaliamma, plucking and savouring wild berries, sharing stories ...

Ammu placed her bag on the half-wall of the ezhuthupura. An eerie silence hung in the air; the birds were silent. The once-lively lake lay frozen and still before her. The chambalpura on the lakeside slope had vanished, reduced to a mere heap of ash. She picked up the hooked rod resting by the cashew tree, with which Kaliamma used to pluck cashews. Ammu poked hard into the ash and tried to stir it up. The ash, which had been hardened by the rain, came loose and started crumbling. She repeatedly poked at the ash heap until she felt exhausted. Her heart ached to know if there were any remnants of Kaliamma; she longed to feel her presence for one last time.

"Did you think there would be no one to perform your last rites? Don't you have me, Mother?" Ammu's voice quivered with emotion. "Have you left us all, leaving no trace of yourself after dedicating your entire life to this place? You spent your life serving others. You loved the earth, the water and all the five elements.

"You cooked for us so we could eat. You tended to the cattle, gathering grass. After completing your chores in the kitchen, you gathered dried leaves in the yard to nourish the trees and the vegetable garden. You placed those leaves at the base of the Gowligathram on the southern and northern ends of the compound, as well as near the plantains. You burned the remaining leaves in the open space on the kadankunnu, mixing the ash with cow dung to make manure for your beloved vegetables.

"But did Kunjikkali, who fed everyone and everything, have to die starving? Or were you forced to leave home? What's the purpose of my existence now?" Ammu agonised, blaming herself.

Kaliamma was never a frail soul paralysed by fear. She always confronted fear head-on, waging war with it. She was the steadfast pillar of Ammu's life. "How could you leave me without a word, just when I was about to finish my work abroad and return to you?" Ammu sobbed, overwhelmed by the pain of loss.

But Vaava had left her first. Perhaps Kaliamma, too, could have complained. Guilt washed over Ammu, and her tears fell onto the pile of ash.

There was no time to lament or dwell on her emotions, Ammu sternly reminded herself. Twilight was approaching, and soon the woods would be enveloped in darkness. Birds were returning to their nests. Some labourers would still be at Paramu Nair's shop in Pallikoodam Mukku (the school junction). They could assist her in breaking apart the blocks of ash with their shovels. Anxious to reach the shop on time, Ammu hurried, navigating the treacherous terrain of stones and thorns before reaching the *anjilichuvadu*. There were seeds scattered around the tree, causing Ammu to slip as she stepped on one. She nearly lost her balance but managed to grasp a vennil vine for support.

The sky darkened as clouds loomed overhead. Strong western winds blew, scattering the dried leaves and making the trees sway. Ammu struggled to see through the swirling dust, feeling immobilised as if her feet were rooted in place. In her moment of distress, she was suddenly enveloped by strong hands, the same hands that had once held her tightly on those nights when she woke up screaming and trembling in fear.

"Vaave," Kaliamma's comforting yet resolute voice echoed in her ears, turning into one of her lullabies once again. Slowly, Ammu drifted into a dream-like slumber.

When she woke up, she found herself at the ezhuthupura, with a saffron flower blooming in the western sky. The blood-red sun was slowly descending into the lake. An eternal lamp burned in the room, and on a teak leaf lay a bone fragment, as if placed for veneration. Kali's chants resonated in her ears, breaking the stillness that settled after the storm.

"Write Vaave, Write..."

Ululating in flames, Kunjikkali embraces death

Epilogue

AMMU CONTINUED TO write until dawn, existing in a state somewhere between a trance and wakefulness.

The tale of Kunjikkali's ululation, even as she was engulfed by flames, was both surreal and strikingly real. Her ululation seemed to echo the voice of the woods, speaking the language of one whose life was intimately intertwined with the earth and water.

She asks, "What right do you have to destroy these forests? These woods were not planted by man; they grew on their own. This forest carries its own scent, songs, and stories. You cannot mould it to suit your convenience."

The language Kali spoke of, that of the forest, lacked the sophistication and embellishments of the educated. Instead, it radiated the freshness of crystal-clear lake water and the sweetness of a nightingale's song.

Kali's dreams thrived within the forest, and her sorrow, like an unquenchable wildfire, continued to spread ...

"Why should Kunjikkali smoulder like an ember lit by another's hand? Abandoned by all, even her own son, why should she keep kindling the fire of despair in her heart? No ... she should become fire, burning with righteous rage and exalt herself high into the skies. Her emancipating flames must be celebrated with ululation..."

Ammu immersing Kaliamma's bone into the sacred waters of the lake

Ammu listened intently to Kunjkkali's fervent words. Was this an auditory hallucination? She pinched herself to ensure she was awake. Deep within, she felt that Kaliamma was urging her to tell her story. So she continued to write.

As the sun, which sets in the west only to rise in the east, slowly opened his eyes and smiled, the pristine lake shed her night-time veil to bask in the warm rays of the sun, beaming in return. The morning breeze carried Kunjikkali's ululation, echoing across and awakening all shores.

The auspicious moment had arrived for Ammu to immerse that piece of Kaliamma's unbent spine, which she had held close to her heart and adorned with wild Indian jasmines, into the holy waters of the lake. Ammu washed her hands, cleansed herself and immersed Kaliamma's bone—an emblem of unwavering self-reliance, self-respect and universal love.

At that sacred moment, Ammu felt an ululation emanating from afar. It echoed like the joyful cry of a bride on her wedding day. From that day onwards, until the end of her days, Kunjikkali's ululation endured—a continuous reminder of all those days she spent fighting against a corrupt system that had perpetually sought to oppress her.

Back then, Ammu hadn't fully grasped the depth and significance of it all. But now, as deep as the Kayalamma (Mother Lake), she could see her Kaliamma closely—frayed by her own life yet dedicated to others. Kaliamma sought to rouse the unjust world, compelling it to heed her piercing cries for change in the decaying old order.

She sensed Kunjikkali's spirit all around her, like water quenching fiery ashes that eventually dissolved in the water...

About the Author

JAYALEKSHMI, a former English teacher at DB College in Sasthamcotta, Kollam, is actively involved in social work, women's issues, and environmental matters. Her contributions include serving as the chairperson of the Kerala State Women's Development Corporation and the Railway Recruitment Board TVC, as well as holding a directorial position at the Rashtriya Mahila Kosh in New Delhi.

She began her writing journey relatively late during the COVID-19 pandemic lockdowns. Being house-bound due to travel restrictions prompted her mind to wander, revisiting and recollecting experiences accumulated over half a century. As a result, she began giving expression to these reflections.

Her first book, a collection of short stories titled *Auld Lang Syne*, was published in May 2022 and received the prestigious 'Madhavikutty Puraskaram'. Her second book, a novel titled *Kunjikkalikkurava*, was published in Malayalam and released at the Sharjah International Book Festival in November 2022. Since then, the novel has garnered positive feedback and appreciation on various social media platforms.

In December 2022, Art Mates UAE, the Pravasi Cultural Organization, presented her with the prestigious 'Puraskaram'. In May 2023, *Kunjikkalikkurava* was honoured with the prestigious 'Dr Sukumar Azhikode Thatwamasi Award' for the best novel of 2022–2023. The book has also been shortlisted for various awards.

Kunjikkalikkurava was translated into English by the author.